The Tall Tales of
Dracula's Daggers

Count Krinkelfiend's Quest

Look out for the sequel!

The Return of the Count

The Tall Tales of
Dracula's Daggers

Count Krinkelfiend's Quest

Gary Morecambe

SCHOLASTIC

Scholastic Children's Books,
Commonwealth House, 1–19 New Oxford Street,
London, WC1A 1NU, UK
A division of Scholastic Ltd
London ~ New York ~ Toronto ~ Sydney ~ Auckland
Mexico City ~ New Delhi ~ Hong Kong

First published in the UK by Scholastic Ltd, 2002

ISBN 0 439 99463 2

Printed and bound in Great Britain by Cox & Wyman Ltd, Reading, Berkshire

10 9 8 7 6 5 4 3 2 1

Contents

An extract from
Professor Erich von Morcumstein's

Guide to Vampires

1. The homeland is the country of
Moldavia, which borders Gotcha, Gertcha
and Rumania.

2. The art of cloaking is the ability to use
metamorphosis to become any animate or
inanimate object. This can only be achieved
by the vampire touching the object in
question, and is one of the most difficult
examples of magic they can perform.

3. Other than exposure to daylight, a stake driven through the heart is believed to be the only way to destroy a vampire for ever.

4. Prince Vlad Basarab III (born in 1431 in Sighisoara, Transylvania) is the full family title of Count Dracula. Indeed, most of the references to Count Dracula I have come across – his castle, his birthplace, life and death – are based on historical fact.

5. It is my belief that Dracula is the first known vampire, and that many have followed but, thus far, escaped the infamy associated with his terrifying reputation.

The view that usually greeted Walter was most certainly tarnished by the unknown caller...

Chapter One

In a Valley Deep and Wide

Ivor Brandt crouched low. Some miles away a village clock struck midnight. Ivor shuddered, and not just because it was a chilly night for the time of year. "At least my teeth aren't chattering," he thought, but that was only because he didn't have very many, and the ones he did have were at opposite ends of his mouth.

He glanced upwards, willing away the thick

clouds that blotted out the moon; his only source of light. He was sure of what he had seen, but as to what was going on. . .

The sound of a muffled voice reached his ears. Could it belong to the figure he'd followed along the ridge? The figure which had seemed to appear from nowhere in the woods and walked downwards into the valley basin? Ivor's curiosity had got the better of him, and he had followed at a safe distance, crossing a brook, struggling with wild brambles and nettles, and ducking behind trees. Now he was settled on a fairly steep incline – waiting; watching; listening.

Without thinking, and Ivor did many things in life without thinking, he half rose to his feet, allowing himself to slither twenty yards down the slippery slope. The trees became fewer the further he descended. Although Ivor wasn't the brightest of creatures, he knew that the trees offered him cover, and that without cover he was vulnerable, so he dug his heels into the soft brown earth and sat back, not risking dropping any lower than was necessary.

Rumour had it that this valley was a dangerous place to be, and Ivor briefly considered turning round and heading for home. His wife, Maryka, and their nine children would be worried about him. He had told her he was only popping out into the valley to chop wood for the fire. That had been three hours ago.

Ivor tensed. Before his eyes, in a clearing fifty yards down the slope, a pile of sticks exploded into flame as if by magic. Things happened quickly. The tall silhouette of a cloaked figure moved silently up to the fire. The figure took a deep breath and began a melancholy chant. Ivor didn't catch the words, but he wouldn't have understood them even if he had.

Nothing happened for a moment, then the tall chanting figure disappeared in a cloud of smoke. When the smoke cleared, all that Ivor could see was a bat flapping about in tiny circles.

Mesmerized, Ivor watched the bat flutter and then shoot off up the valley and over the ridge. All that remained was the glowing embers of the fire. Ivor shook his head in disbelief and started back up the steep slope.

When he reached the ridge and looked back down upon the valley, all was quiet. Had he really seen a man turn into a bat and fly away? The clouds above him parted briefly, allowing the moon to pick out a thin trail of spiralling smoke that clawed for the night sky from far below. "Well, at least the fire was real enough," he said. "Wait till I tell Maryka." As he trundled home, he wondered what she would make of his bizarre findings. But as he trundled home, he was unaware that he was being followed by a large black bat.

The year was 1899. In the tiny mid-European country of Gertcha lived the Gerts. They were a contented people. The years had been kind to them. They had suffered few plagues, even fewer wars, and though the majority might not have had a great deal, they had a quality of life that was enviable.

King Konstantine of Gertcha lived in Viktoria Palace, which stood proudly on the high ground of Solo Summit, looking majestically down upon the centre of Gertcha's principal town, the picturesque Grund.

The king was a man who believed in very little except the wisdom of never shaving. This caused a great deal of trouble, and today was no exception. As he made his way to the terrace, he tripped over the end of his beard and went tumbling across the palace floor. "Stupid floor!" muttered the king. "So deceptively flat."

"Are you all right, Papa?" enquired the king's beautiful daughter, pronouncing "Papa" as "Pap*ar*".

"Oh, fine. Yes, fine, my little one," smiled the king, climbing to his feet.

Since the queen had sadly died some years ago, the king had become dependent on his daughter, Princess Lashka, upon whom he doted utterly.

"Really," she tutted, "that beard should go before you break your neck."

"Oh, but I could never shave it off," he said, and reminded her how long it had taken to grow.

The king's head servant, Walter, entered the room. "You rang, Your Majesty," he stated, bowing.

"Did I?"

"I believe you did, dear Papa," confirmed the princess.

"Oh, right. What was it I wanted?"

"Perhaps something to drink?" she suggested.

"Of course. Something to drink. A nice pot of something hot. Tea will do nicely, er . . . what's your name, again?"

"Walter, Your Majesty."

"Yes, of course it is. And don't you forget it, either."

The head servant bowed again and went to fetch the tea, and the king turned and smiled happily at his daughter. "I think very soon," he mused, "I will call a public holiday. The fine weather is approaching. Our people deserve an extra holiday. It's been a long hard winter for many Gerts, especially those beyond our villages – those toilers of our land."

"Very generous of you, Papa. I will see one is added to the Town Hall calendar at once."

When Walter returned with the twin-spouted teapot, the Princess Lashka passed on the king's wish. "I will send someone to the Town Hall immediately," Walter replied. "Which particular day did His Majesty have in mind?"

"Er. . ." pondered the king.

"Monday," decided the princess for him.

"Excellent, my dear child. What would I do without you?"

Walter wanted to reply that he wouldn't do very much, but naturally said nothing as he slinked away from the terrace.

In the grand hallway, Walter called out to a footman: "Kurt! Go to the Town Hall and register a national holiday for next Monday. His Majesty has seen fit to give everyone a day off. Everyone but us, no doubt."

"Yes, sir."

Kurt made to leave, but as he opened the main doors he was confronted by one of the ugliest people he had ever seen. Briefly they exchanged a few words, and Kurt rushed back inside to speak to Walter.

"There's a man at the door who says he wishes an audience with the king."

"Does he have a card?" sniffed Walter.

"He doesn't even have a jacket," replied Kurt. "And he stinks something rotten."

"Leave him to me."

The beautiful sweeping view that usually greeted Walter on the threshold of the palace was most certainly tarnished by the unknown caller, who was, literally, a blot on the landscape.

"Can I be of assistance, my . . . man?" Walter was going to say, *good* man, but the word stuck in his throat. The man had a lopsided head that was too big for his body.

"Are you the king, then?" chirped the gummy stranger.

"Of course I am not the king. The king does not answer the door dressed as a butler. The king is served. I am one of those employed to serve the king."

"Oh, right. Well, can you serve me up an appointment to see him if he's not too busy?"

Walter tried to remain calm. "The king does not make appointments with just any passer-by. State your business, and in due course it shall be passed on to the king, should his secretary deem it necessary."

"Sounds a bit complicated if you ask me," said the stranger.

"Tell me what your name is," sighed Walter. "You do have one, I assume?

"Oh, yes," said the man. "I have *two*. Ivor Brandt."

"And your business, Brandt?"

"What?"

"The reason for your calling at the royal palace?" said Walter, a sharp edge entering his tone. If it hadn't been for the king's interest in all his subjects, rich and poor, clever and not-so-clever, Walter would have sent this revolting creature packing straight away.

"It's a long story."

"I thought it might be," sighed Walter, "but continue, anyway."

"Well, I was out late last night in Silver Valley collecting logs."

"Stealing logs, you mean."

Ivor shuffled about a little awkwardly. "Well, I only ever take what *I* chop – never anybody else's logs."

"Yes, yes. Hurry up with your story. I haven't got all day."

"Well, down in the valley basin there was a strange-looking man standing near a fire. I had spotted him earlier on, walking along the edge of the ridge in the dark. He was wearing one of those fancy top hats and a black cloak."

"He wore no trousers? He wore no shirt?"

"Of course he did," said Brandt. "I was just giving you a brief description of the chap's appearance to make it more fascinating."

"I see. Continue."

"Being the good citizen I am, I saw it as my duty, if you like, to investigate the goings-on."

"Very diligent of you, I'm sure. Is that all?"

"Not quite. You see, we don't get many strangers hanging around Silver Valley; even fewer singing strange songs."

"What?" said Walter, suddenly interested. This, at least, was something different. "What was this . . . man, singing about, exactly?"

"Meaningless sounds to me," shrugged Ivor. "Then he turned into a bat and flew off."

Walter gawped at Ivor open-mouthed. The man was quite clearly a deranged idiot.

"Yes . . . well . . . thank you very much. I will see your message is duly passed on to the appropriate authority. Goodbye," he said, quickly reaching for the door.

"Er, just doing my duty. . ."

Walter didn't hear the rest of what Ivor was mumbling on about because he had closed the door in his face and hurried off to wash his hands. He did so dislike dealing with peasants. It always left him feeling so unclean.

Ivor began the long, boring descent to Grund, where he'd left his horse and cart. "Didn't even offer me a bean for all that information," he complained bitterly. "All those steps to climb, and for what? Nothing! That's what."

Ivor's journey home was destined to be an extremely long one. As he was heading for the town square, where he'd left his horse and cart, a motorized carriage swerved right in front of him.

"Watch it, you maniac!" bellowed Ivor, shaking a fist.

The driver was full of apologies. "I'm so sorry about that," he grinned, and it was a grin that stretched the entire width of his face. "Thing is, I'm late for an appointment and don't know the area too well."

Ivor was sort of listening, but most of his limited concentration was directed at the gleaming new carriage. What he would do to get rid of his lazy, greedy horse for one of these sleek mechanical machines.

"I'm looking for Fortune Forest," the driver went on, through his fixed grin.

"Nice machine," said Ivor admiringly.

"Er, yes. Perhaps," said the man, "I could take

you for a ride in it, and you, in return, could show me where Fortune Forest is."

"You mean it?"

"Of course."

Ivor jumped in and settled himself beside the driver.

"I saw you coming down the hill from the palace," said the driver, having to shout above the noise of the rushing wind. "Do you work there?"

"Oh no, sir," chortled Ivor. "I was on an important errand. Not that it seems to have done me a lot of good."

"Really?" said the driver, pretending not to be that interested.

"I saw a strange figure the other night," said Ivor. "He was in Silver Valley. Didn't seem quite human, if you ask me."

The driver tried not to grin, but for him that was very difficult. This was certainly the man his paymaster had pursued. "How strange," said the driver.

A few miles later, Ivor shouted, "That's Fortune Forest over there." It eventually ran alongside the road they were following. "That was a great ride.

Thanks," said Ivor. "Now, could you drop me back at my horse and cart?"

The driver didn't answer. He briefly turned to face Ivor and grinned. The track down which they had now turned was muddy and bumpy, and Ivor's misshapen head wobbled like a jelly on a plate.

"I don't think this is the best way back, sir," frowned Ivor, scratching his chin.

"Isn't it?" continued the grinning driver.

Deep in the forest the driver slowed the vehicle, then stopped altogether. Then he switched off the ignition and all was silent, save for the rustling of his hand as he reached in his pocket for a hanky. Ivor hadn't noticed. He was too busy looking nervously all around, and was about to reiterate that this wasn't the right way back, when the handkerchief smothered his nose and mouth. The chloroform worked quickly. Within seconds everything went blurry, and a blanket of darkness swept over him.

The grinning driver started up the automobile again, and turned it round. "That went smoothly. . . Next stop Silver Valley!" he whispered, then he followed the track back on to the main road once more.

13

Amidst the noise of surging passengers there emerged an elderly gentleman.

ᴥ Chapter Two
Enter Von Morcumstein

While poor Ivor was being carted off to a place unknown, a train hooted as it pulled into Grund station.

Amidst the noise of surging passengers there emerged an elderly gentleman. Tall and elegantly dressed, with a deerstalker placed perfectly on his slightly pointed head, he climbed down the steps of his First Class compartment and made for the exit.

Once outside, he was pounced upon by the eager driver sent to collect him. "Professor Erich von Morcumstein?"

"The same."

"I do hope you had a pleasant journey from Germany?"

"Quite pleasant, thank you."

"Our university is looking forward to welcoming you, Professor."

"Glad to hear it, my boy. My visit promises to be much fun, I'm sure."

The driver assisted the famous professor and his single travel bag on to the leather seat at the rear of the open carriage, and draped a rug over the professor's legs. Jumping up to the driver's seat and grabbing hold of the reins, he remarked, "The students are very excited about your lecture on vampire folklore, Professor."

"Folklore *and* history," corrected the professor, before adding, "Good. I shall try not to disappoint them."

"Is it true you have actually met several vampires?"

The professor considered the question carefully,

which was how he considered most questions. "Yes. That is, one or two who claimed they were the Undead of the Night, as we call them. But I have my doubts as to their authenticity. I've yet to meet one who can turn himself into a bat. Now that would certainly be impressive."

They trotted peacefully through the town and into the open countryside. The terrain changed, becoming more rugged the higher they climbed, and the air freshened till it was almost chill.

The driver was keen to engage the professor in conversation. "Have you been to the university before?"

"No," remarked the professor, "but I have read much about it."

"Although the university is called the University of Grund, it is in reality a converted monastery standing in isolation on Marvin's Hill," explained the driver.

"Marvin?" said the professor. "His name is very familiar to me from my studies. Did you know, young man, that it is believed he was an associate of Vlad Basarab the third?"

"Vlad who?" asked the driver.

17

"Vlad Basarab the third," said the professor. "Dracula!"

"Really!" said the driver, but not in a way that suggested for a moment that he believed Dracula had once been a real person. "All we know at the university," he told the professor, "is that Marvin was a blind monk. As you will know, he founded the monastery many centuries ago. It is said he still walks the corridors during the dead of night. The story goes that his body was discovered one day floating in a vat of wine. They used to make a lot of wine in those days, did the monks."

"That does make a good story," said the professor. "However, my own story of Marvin is far more remarkable than that."

"That's not the end of it, Herr Professor," continued the young man. "When they pulled him from the vat they found he had a stake right through his heart. That was what had killed him – *and* the fact he'd drunk most of the wine!" After a longish pause, he added, "More in your line of work, I think." The professor didn't say anything, but he was clearly interested in the tale, because he knew that it was partly true. Only the name of Dracula was missing from the tale. "Some people will believe anything," said the young man, making light of it.

"You should not disbelieve what cannot be explained, my boy," said the professor. "If I had taken that attitude, the world would still believe a true vampire to be a bloodsucking bat with a violent nature."

"And it is not?"

The professor slowly but firmly shook his head. "Only in popular fiction!"

Half an hour later, they turned the final bend, and there astride the hill stood the great iron gates of the ancient university.

Loud chimes from a bell tower rang across a flag-stone courtyard. The professor smiled to himself. It was a wonderfully appropriate setting for a lecture on vampire folklore and history.

The driver jumped down and escorted the professor to his quarters. "You will be called for at seven, Professor. Dinner is served at half past that hour. Feel free to wander around the premises at your will. There is a student art exhibition in the cloisters that may interest you."

"I enjoy art," confessed the professor. "I shall endeavour to go there later."

The professor entered his quarters and walked to the window. In the distance, on a summit, stood a palace, which he recognized as Viktoria Palace, the home of King Konstantine and his beautiful daughter, Princess Lashka. The king, he had read, was a patron of the university.

The professor's gaze wandered from the palace and rested upon a distant valley. A little shudder went down his spine. He knew enough about Transylvania to know how mysterious such valleys could be.

Walter, the king's head servant, was glad it was his night off. It would give him the chance to go into town and dine at his favourite restaurant, Mario's. The stranger who had called at the palace, Ivor Brandt, had unsettled him. He tried for all the world not to think about the scruffy peasant, but the image of a man in a top hat and cape singing a strange song would not leave his head.

"I must be getting old," he decided. "This sort of thing never used to get under my skin."

At the restaurant, Walter was greeted by Mario himself, who was Italian and served the best pizza and pasta in the whole world – or so he claimed. He also grilled a fine steak.

Walter took his favourite table on the verandah and ordered. A few minutes later, Mario returned bearing a large tray. "One cappuccino and cognac fora you, my royala friend," he chuckled, placing the tray on the table. "And the rare steaka, of coursea."

"Thank you, Mario," said Walter. "Good to see you again."

"Anda you, my friend."

As they talked, a man – a tall, stooping man with a fixed grin – sat down at a nearby table.

"Enjoya the meal," said Mario, and he moved to serve his new arrival. Walter sipped his cappuccino and returned to watching the street life.

"A glass of your best vodka," said the man, still grinning.

"Onea vodka comin' up!" said Mario.

Walter acknowledged the grinning man with a curt nod of the head. The man nodded back and continued to grin at Walter, which irritated him enormously. Walter turned away, sipped at his cognac and tried to concentrate on the streets below. But it was difficult. The man's vacant gaze bored right through him.

After a time, Walter turned to him and said, "Do I know you?"

"Me?" grinned the man, looking surprised. "No, I don't think so."

"Then why are you grinning at me?"

"Oh, I am very sorry about that, sir. It's been a problem ever since I was a child. I can't stop grinning at people. Please don't think badly of me. It is an affliction."

Walter shook his head and sighed. "I suppose it's better than being downright miserable, I'll give you that."

"That's very true, sir." He paused, then quickly said, "You work at the palace, don't you?"

Many folk knew that, so the remark didn't particularly surprise Walter.

"Yes, I do. I am head servant to His Majesty."

The man let out a long whistle. "Fancy that. Quite a job, I imagine?"

"It has its moments."

Silence fell. Then the man casually remarked, "Met some character this afternoon who said he'd visited the palace. Didn't say why, though."

Walter slowly turned to him. "Ivor Brandt, you mean?"

"You know him?" said the man with apparent surprise.

"Hardly that," coughed Walter, slightly aghast at the thought. "He called to see the king. Some chance he had of that."

"People will try anything these days. I suppose he was a madman?"

"He was a complete peasant, but I would say that most of his marbles, though in need of considerable dusting, were fairly well in place."

"Chucked him out, I suppose?" pressed the man, but without seeming to press.

"Certainly did. Especially when he started ranting on about seeing a man singing in the valley, and turning. . ." Walter stopped. It sounded too stupid to mention the bat bit.

"Absolutely!" agreed the man from the other table when he realized Walter was not going to expand any further on the matter. "You don't want to take any notice of someone like that. Must be barmy."

Mario brought the gentleman his vodka. The grinning man sat back and took a sip, enjoying the drink all the more now that he had talked with the king's head servant. His paymaster would be highly relieved when he reported back, for unlike the situation with that interfering oaf, Brandt, it appeared drastic measures to keep the king's employee silenced might not be called for. Clearly he had no interest in Brandt and his bizarre story.

But unhappily for the tall, stooping stranger, Walter *did* care about Ivor's little story. His impression of lack of interest was only a poor way to try to convince himself that he should forget all about it. But he just could not, despite all his natural instincts telling him that he should. And his rampant curiosity was about to get him into serious trouble.

On leaving Mario's bar, Walter took a hansom cab to Silver Valley.

At five minutes to midnight, having struggled down a ledge in a similar manner to Ivor Brandt the night before, he spotted the glow of a distant fire. Some while later, Walter reached a suitable spot to lie in wait. He crouched down behind a tree and wondered what on earth he was doing so far from the palace. "I must be as daft as that Brandt creature," he mumbled to himself.

Walter didn't have long to wait before something happened. To his utter astonishment, a tall man dressed in a black top hat and cape emerged from the shadows and stood before the fire. At first he was silent, then the figure raised his chin and began a grim chant. Suddenly it struck Walter what this apparition reminded him of. Silently he murmured the dreaded word "vampire".

Walter felt very cold and frightened. Childhood stories filled his head – of bloodless, lifeless creatures who wore black cloaks and only appeared at night, often to chant ancient incantations. It sent a shiver down his spine.

After a few minutes, Walter decided he had seen enough. But as he made to leave, disaster struck. The part of the slope on which he was perched gave way. He tumbled for what seemed a lifetime, and landed in a muddied and bloodied untidy heap at the foot of the small fire.

The chanting ceased. The tall figure, no more than a black silhouette from where Walter was sitting, turned sharply towards the king's head servant.

"Er, good evening," croaked Walter. "A pleasant evening for a stroll – or a stroll and a song, even!"

The figure moved closer, and in the flickering light, Walter could see that his skin was almost transparent. Every inch of his lean, bloodless body spoke of death.

Quietly, wordlessly, the figure leaned over Walter, then everything went black.

King Konstantine was very agitated. He read the letter again: "You must abdicate the throne in favour of another, who will visit you soon. Acknowledge your acceptance by ringing the clock-tower bells thirteen times at twelve midday. Failure to do so will result in your head servant being returned in several separate deliveries."

The king looked at the bottom of the note. It was signed, "On behalf of royal blood".

"Poor Walter," said the king. "What am I to do? And who could have written this awful note?"

The princess took the letter then pondered a moment. "Do we know how it was delivered?" she asked her anxious father.

"No," he said. "All I know is that one of the servant girls, Karole, brought it to me just a short time ago with the rest of the mail."

"Let us finish our breakfast and consider our next step carefully, Papa. It won't do to make important decisions on an empty stomach."

"Yes, good idea," nodded the king who, short of being in the middle of an earthquake, wouldn't allow *any*thing to come between him and a meal.

After they had finished, the princess rushed off to find Karole. She returned a few minutes later.

"Any news?" asked the king.

"Well, I had a talk with Karole, and it appears this letter was hand delivered by a visitor. She tells me that a grinning man with a stoop called very early and asked that this letter be taken immediately to the king."

"The king being me, of course?" checked the king.

"Yes, of course, Papa. Who else is king?"

"Quite right, my dear. Now don't go forgetting that."

"And Karole," went on the princess, "carried out the instruction unquestioningly. So now, for the sake of poor loyal Walter, you must arrange for the clock to strike thirteen times at twelve."

"If you think that is wise, my child? I don't want to lose my position as king."

"I think it is very necessary to make it look as if we are doing as we are told, even though we have no intention of giving in to this blackmail," she said. "Your late lamented father once said, 'A good king is the servant of his people, and will never let them be endangered if there is anything he can do to prevent it.'" She caught the look of worry in the king's eyes and clasped his hand in hers. "Fear not, dear Papa. Once Walter is safely returned, we can get to the bottom of all this. *And* we will see to it you will always be king, as long as you live."

"Afternoon," chirped Itch, parting his long greasy hair from his eyes and scratching his forearm.

Chapter Three

A Mysterious Disappearance

Loud applause welcomed Professor Erich von Morcumstein as he descended the rostrum in front of two hundred captivated students.

The professor had spoken skilfully on his specialized subject for nearly two hours before answering a whole host of questions. The final question had been, "Is it possible, Professor, that any vampire descendants could be among us today?"

"Very difficult to determine," said the professor. "As you all know, Gertcha's vampire history is non-existent, so the possibility of vampires existing now as, say, they were rumoured to have done in neighbouring Gotcha, is virtually nil. Although I am German, I have spent much of my time in Transylvania. Now, that is a region which, thanks to Vlad Basarab III – better known as Count Dracula – *does* have an ongoing vampire tradition, as I hope I have successfully shown today."

The lecture thus concluded, the professor went to attend a tea party held in his honour on the campus lawns.

Few people noticed the clock-tower bells striking thirteen times at twelve. The king and his daughter did, because they made a point of standing in the ornamental gardens of the palace to listen to them.

"And now, I think, we should wait until sunset," said the princess, in a soft yet decisive voice. "If Walter is not returned to the palace by then, I feel it is our duty to visit the police station and inform them of today's events."

"Er, my thoughts entirely, my child," agreed the king. "But I hope someone doesn't come along claiming they are now the new king. After all, we have just rung the bells thirteen times as asked."

"We are playing a game with them, Papa," smiled the princess, "just as they play a game with us."

"Yes, right."

Walter had not been returned to the palace by sunset.

He had not been returned an hour after sunset, either.

"Time for the police, Papa," announced the princess. "I will summon the royal carriage straight away."

Inspector Klaw listened thoughtfully as Princess Lashka explained the events which had led to this rare visit to the Grund police station. When she had finished, he confessed to being most alarmed by the report. "So, your servant has been kidnapped, you say?"

"Yes," nodded the king.

"A threatening letter, you say?"

"Yes," nodded the king.

"Can I see it?"

The king shuffled with embarrassment. "Er, His Majesty," explained the princess, "had a slight accident with the letter, Inspector."

"I thought it was a flannel, and I washed my face with it," the king admitted. "Stupid mistake, but I'd left it by my toothbrush. Sorry."

There followed a moment's pause, then the inspector said, "Quite understandable, Your Majesty. An easy mistake to make. Anyway, the important thing is your servant has not been returned."

"That's right," said the king, "and after we rang the bells thirteen times at midday as requested."

The inspector solemnly shook his head and rested his hands on his knees while he thought about how to proceed. He hadn't been an inspector for very long. He was a young man who had climbed the ranks quickly. This was his first case, "And *what* a first case," he was nervously thinking.

"It would appear to me, Your Highnesses," he told

them at length, "that someone's been giving you the runaround: checking to see how much interest you have in this head servant of yours. You've shown them your hand now, which is a pity. They know you care a great deal about him."

"Well, I, er. . ." faltered the king awkwardly. "I do care about him. Also, I care about being . . . being. . ."

"The king!" finished his daughter.

"Yes. That, too!" said the king. "I don't know who is trying to take my throne, but they're not going to do it while *I* am king. And I *am* king. My daughter reminded me of that only this morning."

"Inspector," said Princess Lashka, "if their threat was serious, they are planning to return our head servant by the pound."

"They still might, Ma'am," pointed out the inspector, and that thought made the king and his daughter most uncomfortable.

"However," said the inspector, "it was Walter's night off last night. Somebody might have seen or heard something. It is a good starting point. I would suggest you return to your palace and await news.

I will get to work and report any findings to you directly, if that suits Your Majesty?"

"Eh?" said the king.

"That would be perfect," said the princess. "And I'm sure you will do your best to find our head servant, Inspector."

King Konstantine and Princess Lashka returned to the palace. The inspector, accompanied by a couple of officers, went into town to begin making enquiries. This eventually brought them to Mario's.

"Whatsa thata you saya?" gasped Mario. "Mya royal friend isa keednapped?"

"You know this Walter?"

"Knowa him?" laughed Mario. "He wasa here lasta nighta havinka drink and a bitea to eata."

"Did he talk with anyone?"

"Yeh – he talka with me."

"I meant anyone *else*," explained the inspector.

"Nah, nobody else. Wait. There was a mana at anudder table. Walter, he likea the peacenquiet. This udder mana was a bit of a nuisance. He keepa smiling ata Walter, like he swallowed a cucumber sideaways."

"You would recognize this man if he showed up again?"

"Sure I woulda," said Mario. "He givea me the creeps."

"Be sure you call me the moment you see him again."

"For Walter, I'da do anything."

Inspector Klaw moved on, feeling a little heartened but not wholly satisfied. Knowing Walter's movements on the night in question was useful, but unless this mystery stranger showed himself again, his investigations could grind to a halt.

When the inspector arrived back at his office, there was a woman waiting to speak with him.

"Can I help you, madam?" he asked wearily, as he made a quick, unconscious study of her. Her rough hands and ruddy cheeks suggested she led a hard outdoor life.

"Oh, I do hope so, Inspector," said the woman very anxiously. "It's my husband, Ivor. He's gone missing!"

37

The tall stooping stranger with the fixed grin was, in fact, a criminal called Vermyn, and at that precise moment he was sitting inside his cave-like hideout in Fortune Forest. No one could possibly find it – not even if they were to stumble accidentally into that part of the forest – for the entrance was covered in bracken and branches threaded together. Inside, there was nothing but a table and some chairs. A circle of ashes glowed on the mud floor marking the remains of a fire. Every now and then, he would toss a stick upon them, just to keep the fire alight. It was cosy and secure, though a little smoky.

Vermyn's planning had been somewhat upset by the interfering head servant to the king. He was angry with himself for having misjudged Walter. He had been absolutely positive that the man had no interest whatsoever in Ivor Brandt's story. However, his employer had made it very plain to him that Walter had plenty of interest in Brandt's story. And now Walter, too, was a captive – a hostage. Things had been happening quickly of late, but Vermyn prided himself on being a quick thinker.

Suddenly, from just outside his hideout, came a thick, raspy voice. "Friend or foe, heel or toe, let me in or I shall go!"

Vermyn recognized the voice without having to listen to the whole password – or passrhyme, to be precise. "Enter, Itch or Scratch – whichever one you are," he said, moodily.

Itch and his brother Scratch took a last furtive look around them before brushing back a portion of the bracken cover and entering Vermyn's den.

"Afternoon!" chirped Itch, parting his long greasy hair from his eyes, and scratching a bare part of his forearm that his tatty old jacket didn't quite cover.

"Yes. A good afternoon to one and all, this merry day," added Scratch.

"Close the door and sit down!" ordered Vermyn. "I hope you ensured you were not followed here?"

"You can count on us for discretion," said Itch.

"Oh yes, for discretion you can count on us," agreed Scratch, who also began scratching himself, but on the back of his neck, where he had a large purple boil.

The brothers were quite similar to look at; large

but not fat, and with the one noticeable difference that Scratch was about three inches taller than his brother.

"What kept you?" Vermyn asked sternly.

"We were busy doing what you wanted," said Itch.

"That's right," confirmed Scratch. "We've been moving innocently around the town keeping our eyes open for anything interesting."

"And?" encouraged Vermyn.

Itch had a sly glint in his eyes. "A few more kronks and we may be able to update you on the latest. Nothing in this world comes free. You should know that, Vermyn."

Vermyn reached in his pocket and tossed them a couple of coins each. "And that's full payment," he told them sharply, his fixed grin not nearly so fixed.

"We were near the high street in town," said Scratch. "We were just about to leave to make our way here, when. . ."

". . .we caught sight of a certain Inspector Klaw," finished Itch.

"So what?" shrugged Vermyn.

"He was making enquiries about your royal hostage."

"Our hostage is not of royal descent," corrected Vermyn, "he merely works for the royal family. However," he admitted, "you have done well. It appears I was quite correct in supposing the king would be protective of one of his employees."

"The king must be a very caring man," said Itch. "Unlike this old count of yours."

"Enough!" snapped Vermyn. "I told you before not to call him that. He is our paymaster, and nothing more." He sighed heavily. "Tonight I am due to make a report to the cou— to our paymaster." Itch and Scratch both sniggered at his near slip up. "I shall include your findings. And meanwhile," he said, staring them coldly in the eyes, "you will hold your tongues. If I hear that you've failed to do so, then you can be sure *He* will see to it you have no tongues left to hold. Is that clear?"

For the first time the two brothers looked nearly serious. "Er, OK," mumbled Itch. Scratch said nothing, but continued to pick at a wart which had been on his left thumb for as long as he could recall.

"Good. Now leave," said Vermyn, gesturing at the door. "I will contact you again shortly. In the meantime, you know your duties."

"No chance of a bonus?" asked Scratch.

"You are quite right," grinned Vermyn. "There is no chance of a bonus." He laughed madly at his little joke. The brothers frowned, but they slipped away without another word.

Vermyn made himself a pot of tea and brooded over the operation in hand.

"So, not only did the bells toll thirteen times in response to my letter, but they have called in our good police force. Walter is turning out to be an excellent, if accidental, hostage. Certainly better than that misfit who visited the palace. But I must take full advantage of both our hostages. I must view them as a help and not a hindrance." His thoughts turned momentarily to the count. "If I don't," he added, "then I might end up in the same position as them."

Vermyn thought about King Konstantine. There was little likelihood of inducing his abdication. And he was in no doubt that the count would be of similar mind.

He poured himself another cup of tea and started contemplating his next visit to the count's lair. He had made the decision long ago not to trust anyone. Not even the count. Do the job, take the money and run, was the best bet.

Inspector Klaw asked Maryka Brandt to repeat her story, keeping to the facts and discarding the irrelevant bits. When she reached the part about Silver Valley, he interrupted her. "The figure your husband described. Did he wear a black top hat as well as a cape?"

"I think that's what he said. Thing is, I was that annoyed with him for being late for his dinner, I was hardly listening. And my Ivor never talks much when I'm beating him with a wooden spoon."

"So I can imagine."

"Of course, the bit about turning into a bat made my ears prick up, like I told you, but I thought he might have stopped at the local on the way home."

"I'm sorry?"

"Fuelled himself up on a few jugs of the local brew. *Fantasized* it all, Inspector."

"Ah, yes. Right. Including the appearance of the . . . the bat?"

"What's so strange about a bat?" sighed Maryka. "We see bats every night, everywhere, don't we Inspector?"

"I suppose we do," he smiled, weakly.

"Do you think my Ivor's story is important, Inspector?" asked Maryka Brandt. "Do you think he's in *real* trouble?"

The inspector rubbed his eyes. "What was that? Important? In trouble? Er, yes, it could be so, Mrs Brandt." He stood up and ushered her out through the door. "Now, I want you to go home with one of my officers, Mrs Brandt. He will stay and guard you and your family until your husband has been safely returned."

"Is my Ivor in some sort of serious danger, then?"

"I can't tell you any more at present, Mrs Brandt. There is something important that needs to be verified before I can answer any more questions."

Before Maryka Brandt could *ask* any further questions, Klaw slammed the door and picked up the telephone. He dialled a number and waited.

"Is that the university? Good. I read that Professor von Morcumstein, the authority on vampirism, is visiting. Is he still there?" A short pause. "Excellent. Tell him I need to speak to him at once. Who am I? I am Inspector Klaw of the Gertcha police department in Grund." Another short pause. "Yes, I know it's very late, but this is a matter of great urgency."

The inspector waited as requested. A few minutes later, he heard muffled voices on the other end of the line, and someone coughing.

"Hello?" said a crackling voice.

"Professor von Morcumstein?"

"Yes. And you are Inspector Klaw?"

"That is correct, sir. Could you come at once to my office, Professor? I have a problem that might well be of interest to you. It's to do with . . . vampires."

"I see," said the professor. "Then I suppose I must come."

The professor replaced the receiver and turned to the tutor. "Could you arrange for me to be taken to the police station in Grund?"

"Certainly, Herr Professor."

A few minutes later, he was on his way. The hansom cab sped down the winding track towards Grund where Inspector Klaw awaited him. Wearily, Professor von Morcumstein entered the police station.

"Good evening, Inspector," said the professor, tilting his hat in a stiff, formal fashion as he entered Inspector Klaw's office. Klaw didn't have to be psychic to see that as far as the professor was concerned it was anything *but* a good evening. "This diversion has meant an interruption to an otherwise early night for me, in preparation for an even earlier start back home tomorrow morning," said the professor. He levelled his gaze at the inspector. "This had better be good, my friend!"

When Inspector Klaw had finished, the professor sipped delicately at the glass of orange juice he had requested. "I must say, it is very interesting. Of course, it could all prove harmless enough, but add the mystery of the nocturnal chanter in the valley to the sudden disappearance of two local men, and there are distinct possibilities." He added, tapping

A Mysterious Disappearance

his head, "I keep a mass of information in here, both interesting and exceedingly uninteresting. I know, for instance, that previous sightings of vampires have not differed much in report from the one supplied by the wife of this missing man. Chanting; fires; dark clothes; top hats; always during the dead of night. And bat-like apparitions. That one comes up with incredible regularity. Definite – some would say, *conclusive* – similarities."

"So you believe, however fantastic it sounds, and it sounds extremely fantastic to me," said Inspector Klaw, "that this Ivor Brandt and the king's head servant, Walter, have become victims of . . . of a vampire?"

"This is the big question, Inspector," said the professor. "It is possible. You definitely did the correct thing in contacting me, in spite of my train having to depart without me. I do apologize if I seemed a little ruffled on my arrival."

"No apology necessary, Professor. I had heard you were in Grund as part of your lecture tour. Indeed, were it not for work, I was contemplating attending your lecture at the university myself."

"As a believer or an unbeliever?" smiled the professor.

"An unbeliever who perhaps would like to believe," said Klaw.

"And so maybe the opportunity arises through this case you have, yes?"

"Maybe."

"Then I hope my support will be of assistance."

Klaw gently nodded. "I'm greatly in need of support in this matter. I have reports to make for my superior. If I write, 'Am presently engaged in searching for a kidnapping vampire', I think I might just lose my job."

"I see. But if you mention you have consulted me. . .?"

"Exactly, Professor. Your knowledge and experience are held in the deepest respect in Gertcha. My superior, though a realist, takes much interest in what academics have to say. He definitely would not dare question your opinions – not immediately, that is."

"Then let us make a little toast to our success."

They raised their glasses. "To our success," they said in unison.

"And to the tracking down of all vampires," added the professor, cheerfully.

The inspector raised his glass again but said nothing. If there really was a vampire in Silver Valley, he wasn't as enthusiastic as the professor about confronting it.

"Good morning, gentlemen," said the count.

◥ Chapter Four
Hideaway

Though restless, Vermyn obeyed instructions and waited until after midnight before following the secret trail into Silver Valley. He knew the route well. He made it his job to know the quickest, safest routes to *all* his paymasters, and the count was only one of many to whom he'd offered his talents. Mind you, he was the first vampire Vermyn had ever had dealings with: not that the count had ever admitted to being a vampire in so many words. But the clues were there. The translucent skin, the meetings after dark, the strange clothes, the unusual hideout. They were hardly the hallmarks of your average Gertcha citizen. But Vermyn didn't really care. He would deal with the devil himself if it meant more kronks in his hands.

An owl hooted as Vermyn approached a gully that led to a tiny brook. He could hear the soft tinkling of water long before setting eyes upon it. Loose stones crunched underfoot as he forged a way across, then it was a treacherous climb up the bank on the far side, his damp soles slipping in the mud like skates on ice. The darkness and foliage seemed to close in on him, and he knew he was getting close.

When he reached the foot of a large oak tree, his familiar cunning grin returned. He had arrived. He tapped twice on the tree as if it were a door – which in a way it was.

Slowly the base of the tree slid open, and he stepped inside. At once it closed behind him as, simultaneously, flaming torches jutting out from smooth curved walls illuminated a long descending tunnel ahead. Vermyn blinked several times as he adjusted to the sudden brightness, then followed the tunnel downwards into the count's secret lair.

The count didn't like visitors, but Vermyn had been quick to see how valuable he was to the success of the count's plan – not that he knew the full details of what that plan itself was. His greatest use was that, unlike the count, he could go out into the daylight world.

Vermyn reached the bottom of the long tunnel. The air was thin and sour, and he found it difficult to breathe. He felt, rather than saw, a presence in the chamber.

"You have come," stated a deep booming voice.

The count emerged from behind a pillar. He was tall; well over six feet. Vermyn thought he looked like someone who had gone to a lot of trouble for a fancy dress party, and for this reason he had never found him as frightening as he perhaps might have done. Or, indeed, should have done.

"Come hither into the dying room," commanded the count. Vermyn was used to the count's strange choice of words and phrases. The dying room was, of course, the living room. The dissection room was the kitchen. The mortuary, the bedroom, and so on.

The room was small and badly lit; just the miserable sort of atmosphere the count enjoyed. "Be seated, mortal one." The count sat down on the floor and crossed his legs. Vermyn grinned, shrugged, and did the same. "What goes on in the daylight world?" asked the count.

"Things are going well, Your Countship," he replied. "The palace is pleasingly concerned with the disappearance of its head servant, and—"

"I do not like all this confusion that is developing," the count calmly interrupted – so calmly that Vermyn wondered if he'd been listening at all. "My nightly pleasure of a walk along the ridge, followed by a song in front of a fire before going off hunting has had to stop because of the interest it appears to be causing. If this continues, I will end up as a tourist attraction." He pointed threateningly at Vermyn. "My taking over the palace, followed by the whole of Gertcha and Gotcha and, given time, all central and eastern Europe, should have been a relatively simple process for someone with my powers. Now, it would seem, interference from others, plus general incompetence all round, is hampering my plans. My powers are being stretched from all directions and without them I cannot hope to see my ambitions fulfilled. I thought I'd made it plain at the outset that I wished for my move from this hideout to the palace to be carried out with smooth precision. Surely soon the king will abdicate, and I will occupy the palace in his place."

"I'm sure you will, Count," said Vermyn, but he didn't think that it was very likely. "But more important, Count, is that no one has any leads to your hideout here."

Vermyn's words did little to reassure Count Krinkelfiend.

"Except that I am host to a member of the royal staff," the count reminded him, "and, far worse, to a particularly odious creature who has difficulty even in recalling his own name." He clenched his fists into tight balls. "I am beginning to regret my suggestion that you bring this . . . this. . ."

"Ivor Brandt, Your Countship," finished Vermyn.

"This Ivor Brandt, to my dwelling. It had seemed a good idea at the time, when I first caught him spying on me."

"Oh, yes, Your Countship," grovelled Vermyn. "An excellent idea. And he *had* been talking with the king's head servant, so he could have been trouble."

"He *is* trouble," sighed Count Krinkelfiend. "He is a pain in the. . ."

He left the sentence unfinished, but his point had been made.

"Unlike Brandt, the king's servant is important," Count Krinkelfiend went on. "His disappearance causes interest. While it is hoped such interest benefits us in the long-term, in the short-term it causes me discomfort. How long before the police come searching this valley? Answer me that."

"Er, well. . ."

"Perhaps a little torture followed by transformation into something more appropriate to his intellect would be suitable for Brandt," the count said suddenly, changing the subject – much to the relief of Vermyn. "What say you, my quiet friend?"

"Why not?" gulped Vermyn.

There was a short silence, just long enough for Vermyn to ponder on what sort of "something" the count might have in mind for Brandt. Then the count rose smoothly to his feet and headed for the door. "Leave me your usual written report and go. You will be contacted when required. In the meantime, I do not wish for further visitors to my part of the valley, and I especially do not wish for any more hostages, accidental or otherwise. I presume I make myself plain?"

"Entirely, Your Countship," said Vermyn, though he thought it a bit unfair: it hadn't been entirely *his* fault. Then he drew a deep breath and said, as if it was a mere afterthought, "Oh, there is the little matter of wages."

Count Krinkelfiend stopped and slowly turned to him.

"Very well," he said at length. "Five hundred kronks will be delivered to your place of rest in Fortune Forest."

"Anything you say, Your Countship," bowed Vermyn, grinning his biggest grin yet. Then he took out his written report, placed it on a table and left.

Count Arnold Krinkelfiend made his way to a small room connected to the one in which they had been talking. Inside, an iron cage hung from the ceiling, and in the cage were two men.

"Good morning, gentlemen," said the count.

"It is still night time for us mortal creatures," said Walter, defiantly.

"We work on VT here," sneered the count, as he moved closer to the cage. "That's Vampire Time. Now, would you care for someone to eat? I should hate to think my guests were going hungry."

"I'm not hungry," snubbed Walter.

"I wouldn't mind a sandwich," smiled Ivor Brandt.

Walter looked at him with disgust. This was his punishment for being so inquisitive. To share a cell with this deformed fool had to be a fate worse than death.

"Ham with a little mustard would be nice," Ivor added.

"I can only offer you pickled rat for the moment," sneered the count.

"That'll do fine," Ivor called out.

"Well you'll just have to wait!" said the count,

tiring of the conversation. Then he swept out of the room, his black cloak quivering in his trail.

Ivor turned to Walter and said, "A nice man, that."

"How can you eat at a time like this?" hissed Walter.

Brandt, who took the question seriously, said, "I suppose, because I'm hungry."

The count hurried along to his private chamber. He massaged his thin hands against each other, then delicately reached for a large book on a shelf.

He placed the book on the desk and turned to a marked page. His face burst into a smile, and for a second he looked almost human.

There was a small illustration of a dagger in a sheath: a quite stupendous dagger, which almost glittered on the page. Beneath the illustration were the following words: "The dagger pictured above was commissioned by Vlad Dracula, while visiting Gertcha in 1451, and is the work of Marvin, the blind monk of Grund."

For a few moments, the count stroked the illustration with his fingertips. "Soon you will be mine," he whispered. Then he slammed the book shut with finality and moved on to other matters. Itch and Scratch sat down on a park bench and unwrapped two sandwiches they'd bought at Krusts, the bakery.

"Mine was cheese, yours ham," said Itch, quickly switching them round.

"Ham!" groaned Scratch. "I thought I asked for *jam*!"

"Too bad," laughed Itch. He took a hungry bite of his cheese sandwich and winced. "Ugh! Stale as year-old eggs."

"Ha! ha!" said Scratch, returning the scorn. "Hard cheese, I believe they say."

"Give us a nibble of your ham. Go on, Scratch. Please, please, please."

"Not likely. You wouldn't have given me a bite of your cheese one."

"I would."

"Yes, you would now, cos it's mouldy. You wouldn't have done otherwise."

"I would."

"Wouldn't."

"Would."

"Wouldn't."

This futile argument might have continued long into the afternoon had they not simultaneously glimpsed their prey heading through the park.

In accordance with Vermyn's wishes, they had continued to track Inspector Klaw. This had been easy, though exceedingly boring. Klaw didn't appear to do anything of interest. Spying him in deep discussion with someone as he ambled by the lake some thirty yards from where they were sitting was the most exciting moment of their pursuit.

"I'm sure I've seen that face before," remarked Itch.

"Of course you have," said Scratch. "We've been following it for the last twenty-four hours."

"Not Klaw, you fool. The other man."

"No," said Scratch, shaking his head. "Doesn't ring any bells for me."

Suddenly Itch snapped his fingers. "Got it! He's that famous German lecturer. I read about him coming here to do a talk."

"I didn't know you could read!"

"I can't."

"Well how did you read about him, then?"

"Well," explained Itch, "I saw a notice outside the Town Hall next to a mugshot of the professor over there. I said to someone standing nearby, 'Fancy that then. Most interesting.' They, of course, replied, 'Yes. Professor Erich von Morcumstein coming to our tiny country to make a speech on vampires at the university. Most interesting.' That's the way I get most of my information when it's in writing."

"Vampires!" mused Scratch. "That's going to interest Vermyn, wouldn't you say?"

"I should say so. Could be worth a kronk or two bonus, a piece of information like that."

"Could also mean a headache for this count chap in Silver Valley," said Scratch.

"You mean, 'Mr Paymaster'," said Itch, doing a poor impression of Vermyn. "Anyway," he went on, "we don't know for sure there *is* a count. We only have Vermyn's word for it, and I wouldn't trust him any more than I trust . . . well, us!"

"He exists, all right," smiled Scratch. "I can tell when Vermyn is speaking the truth. He stops grinning. And furthermore," he added, "I reckon there's more to this count than Vermyn admits.

Have you noticed how twitchy he gets whenever we mention his name?"

"That's true," said Itch. "So, what are we going to do?"

Scratch tapped the side of his nose. "What we're going to do, little brother, is decide how we're going to play our hand."

"How do you mean?"

"We could make substantial gain from our dear police department were we to take our news to them. For instance, who else knows where Vermyn hides? And he's the link to the mysterious old count, is he not?"

"Yeah – and I don't like Vermyn," said Itch, meaningfully. "So what's the plan of action?"

"There's time yet," replied Scratch. "So we'll do what we always do. We'll wait for our opportunity, and when it comes. . ." He smiled knowingly.

"We'll mess it up?" suggested Itch.

"No, we won't mess it up," said Scratch irritably. "We'll take that opportunity to make ourselves rich."

As he eased open the door Max prepared himself for
the frenzy of excitement that would follow.

ᴥ Chapter Five
Son of a Count

In a notably picturesque part of Grund stood an ornate, whitewashed building, reserved entirely for the convenience of His Majesty. Today, the king and his daughter, Princess Lashka, were having a meeting there with Professor von Morcumstein and Inspector Klaw.

"We are making some headway in this matter, Your Majesty," said Klaw. "We believe, for instance,

that there could be a link between the disappearance of your head servant, Walter, and the sighting
. . . the sighting of a vampire."

"A vampire?" cried the king.

The princess seemed unperturbed. "And so,
Professor," she said, turning away from Klaw to
face von Morcumstein. "We are told you know all
about vampires?"

"As much, if not more, than any other man,
Ma'am," he acknowledged with a gracious bow of
his head.

"I see. And you think it is a vampire who has
kidnapped our head servant, Walter?" she said.

"This is possible," nodded the professor. "There
is a historical link in this general region with
vampirism." The princess looked far from
convinced, and the king muttered something about
how difficult it was to get by without a decent
head servant.

"If I could see the abductor of your servant, Your
Majesty," said the professor, turning to the king, "I
might – I *would* – recognize him for what he
really is."

Klaw rested a hand on the professor's shoulder. "Our learned friend," he told them, "has been studying his various books this afternoon. He has traced a line of vampires from our neighbouring country of Gotcha. Direct cousins to the family of King Victor and Queen Valeeta."

"I'm not sure I know them," muttered the king. "Do *they* know *me*?"

"This was a long time ago, Your Majesty," explained Klaw. "Many doubted they were even of vampire blood. All that sort of thing was hastily covered up at the time."

"Do you therefore think, Professor," asked the princess, "that the person responsible for the abduction is descended from these . . . vampires?"

"This is merely speculation, Ma'am," warned the professor, "but it is possible that it is a Krinkelfiend we are seeking. At my home in Muhlhausen, I have recorded various family trees. The Krinkelfiend line comes directly from King Victor and Queen Valeeta." The professor shook his head a few times and said, almost to himself, "If I was to try and pinpoint the identity

67

of this vampire, I would place Count Arnold Krinkelfiend high on my list. Though this count has not been seen for years – and never in daylight – he has been known to have an eccentric lifestyle. Not conclusive in itself, but curious in view of what we are now witnessing. Certainly, no other names immediately spring to my mind."

"Vampires, eh?" muttered the king, rubbing his hands. "Sounds interesting. They're the chaps who bite your neck after dark, aren't they?"

The princess ignored her father's comments. "Can a search of his castle be made? In the circumstances I would have thought that a reasonable request."

"Reasonable? Perhaps so, Ma'am," said the professor, "but at the same time unhelpful. If there were the remotest signs that indicated the count was an active vampire, it would only confirm what I, at least, already believe to be likely. It would have little bearing on the outcome of our current situation. Also, it might serve to alert him."

Klaw, who was not immune to the young

princess's beauty, surrendered to her wishes. "I suppose it would do no harm for me to arrange with the GPD to send someone round to make a discreet enquiry, if it so pleases you, Your Highness."

"What about, er, Walter?" said the king, confused by all this sidetracking. "What's being, er, done about him? Terrible nuisance having no head servant, you know!"

"We are making a little progress, Your Majesty," said Klaw. "I'm acting on a small piece of information that came my way, thanks to the wife of the missing Ivor Brandt, and have arranged to lead a small team of men on a special search mission that will take us right across Silver Valley. At the very least we might discover what mystery lies there."

Sergeant Klubb of the GPD was given the assignment of visiting Count Arnold Krinkelfiend's Castle Windfall, near Clapem in neighbouring Gotcha. It was a small castle as mid-European castles went, but it had a certain Gothic charm which didn't pass unnoticed by the young policeman.

There was no reply when he knocked at the door, so he began hunting round the grounds and finally came across someone hoeing a lettuce patch in a vegetable garden.

"Just a few questions, sir," smiled the sergeant, flashing his identity card.

The gardener stopped hoeing and looked warily at the policeman.

"Who are you, exactly, sir?" the policeman asked.

The man blinked a few times, looked at his hoe and said, "I'm the gardener."

"Er, yes . . . right," said Klubb, writing down the reply.

'The owner of this fine property, one Count Arnold Krinkelfiend: away is he, sir?"

"Yes," nodded the gardener. "He's on vacation in Bulgaria for a few weeks. Business, I believe."

"I see. And you have regular contact with your employer when he's around, do you, sir?"

"What a peculiar question, Sergeant."

"Just doing my duty, sir."

"I see him from time to time," said the gardener.

"We don't stop to chat, as I am merely his gardener. Nothing more, nothing less."

"I see."

"Is there anything else, Sergeant? I do have the gardens to tend."

"I would like to know if there is any family, sir. Any you know of, that is."

"I . . . I believe there is a son," said the gardener. "I haven't met him, though."

The sergeant thanked him and snapped shut his notebook. "Let's hope the good weather lasts, sir. Have an enjoyable day."

The gardener watched the sergeant from the corner of his eye as he moved to the castle and peered through the ground-floor windows.

When the sergeant's trap had crunched down the drive, the gardener rummaged in his pocket for a key. Feeling more than a little ruffled, he turned the lock of the front door and hurried inside.

It was dark and musty. The gardener lit a match and stumbled towards a table where a half-consumed candle stood in a silver candelabrum.

Soon the room was awash with flickering light.

He turned to face an enormous cupboard. It never failed to amaze him how big this cupboard was, even though he'd seen it many times.

As he eased open the door he prepared himself for the frenzy of excitement that would follow. The appearance of someone always did that, especially near feeding time.

Squawking and screeching noises echoed in the air, as he quickly cast an eye across the rows of tiny cages that ran the length of four shelves. Each cage had something in it. One had a parrot, another a rat; and there was a rabbit, a cat, a mole, a guinea pig, a lizard, a chicken, a porcupine, a viper . . . and a bat.

Carefully he removed the cage with the bat and closed the cupboard door behind him. He took it over to the table and gently placed it down.

The bat squeaked a few times and flapped its wings. The gardener hoped it wasn't too angry with him. The wire door on the cage opened easily, and he stood back and waited.

The bat flew out, circled the room several times

then landed upside-down on the floor a few feet from its cage.

A loud bang, a puff of purple smoke and the bat was no longer a bat, but Count Arnold Krinkelfiend. A tall, dark and upside-down Count Arnold Krinkelfiend, with a black top hat and cloak.

"Is it midnight, Max?" the count enquired from his extraordinary position.

"No. It's mid-afternoon, but. . ."

"What on earth are you doing disturbing me in the middle of the day, Max? Have you taken leave of your senses? I've busy nights ahead of me."

"It's important, Your Lordship," the gardener quickly said, and he told him of the visitor they had just had.

"So, the Law of Gertcha is now visiting my home in Gotcha," grumbled the count.

He turned over and climbed stiffly on to his long legs. "Yes, this is interesting. Indeed, you were right to wake me."

"Oh, thank you: most kind, Your Greatness."

"And as it was, I was tiring of conversation in the cupboard."

"Who were you talking to, Your Magnificence?"

"The old Archbishop of Gotcha. He was becoming far too inquisitive."

"He is the rat, isn't he sir?" Max tried to recall.

"No. The rat is the former mayor. Unfortunately for him he disagreed with me over taxation. As you are aware, I hate anyone disagreeing with me over taxation. Now, he sits in his cage sulking. Huh! You would have thought it was *my* fault."

"Silly mayor," said Max. The count hated anyone disagreeing with him over anything, and that was why the cupboard was full of once-important people whom he had turned into a curious collection of pets.

The count stretched out his long arms and yawned. "I so enjoy returning home for my rest. I cannot recommend living beneath forest trees in an unfamiliar valley. This cupboard has become home to me, Max."

"Yes, of course, Your Eminence," said Max. "Though not quite like our old home, sir."

The count quivered at the words "old home". "You are right, Max. One day, we will return to the homeland. We will return to Transylvania, home of our beloved Master, and it will be like the old times, yes?"

"Most surely, sir, most surely."

"And now, I intend to rest for a little longer," said the count, "then at midnight, I will fly back over to Silver Valley and ponder over this new problem."

"Very good, sir," said the gardener. "I'll be sure to wake you."

With that, the count transmogrified into a bat and returned to his cage.

Silver Valley was in for a busy night. Max had woken the count at midnight as requested and now he was winging his way towards his lair. Inspector Klaw and his entourage were making tracks through the long grass in every direction but the right one; and Itch and Scratch were observing their progress from a tree on the ridge.

As the count landed at the entrance to his lair, he simultaneously returned to human form. Once safely inside, he began pacing up and down. He

75

couldn't recall the last time a representative of the police department had taken time to pay his home a visit.

"It seems they know all about me," he whispered to himself. "But they'll never stop me," he added, as if it were a matter of fact. "Very soon my plan will enter its second phase – the takeover of Grund, with particular reference to Viktoria Palace. Then the whole of middle Europe will know what has happened, and I will be recognized as king of Gertcha." He savoured the thought a moment.

"Well, thanks for that. I wondered what your plan was," said a voice from the darkness.

In a flash, the count spun around, his arms raised, a magic spell flickering on the very tips of his fingers. Then he saw his son. "Rupert!" gasped the count. "I almost turned you into something extremely unpleasant." They moved towards each other. "It has been a long time, my former son."

Count Krinkelfiend had disowned his son some years earlier. This was because Rupert was only half vampire, his late mother having been a mortal being. Not that Rupert, unlike his father, saw that as a weakness. Indeed, the fact that he was half human, and cared about people, was a great strength.

"You were not so careless as to be followed here, I hope?" asked the count.

"Like you, I flew here. And no one is going to follow a bat."

"Yes, that is probably so, my former son. But tell me," said the count, narrowing his eyes, "how did you find me?"

"My castle is not that great a distance from yours, Father. And as you have been receiving a lot of attention just lately, I decided to check up on you."

"Very cunning, my former son," acknowledged the count. "You might make a complete vampire, yet." The count patted his son's shoulder. "But let us not bother ourselves unduly with the bungling efforts of the police. They will never find this hideout. We must dine together. The night is yet young and there is so much for us to discuss. I want you to be my chief secretary when the

77

Krinkelfiend name echoes far and wide from Viktoria Palace."

"So that's what all this is about," said Rupert, folding his arms. "Dreams of empire-building again, eh Father?"

"When I seize power, it will be the greatest moment since King Victor and Queen Valeeta reigned supreme," he told Rupert.

While this mournful reunion was taking place, Inspector Klaw was studying his singed and torn clothes. With only oil-fired lanterns to guide them, an easy descent had been impossible. One of the officers, in his nervousness, had followed the inspector a little too closely, and the flame from his lantern had set fire to Klaw's trousers. What with the difficult terrain as well, Klaw knew it was to be a long and exhausting night.

Itch and Scratch were equally as fed up. Itch passed his brother the field glasses. "Pathetic!" he groaned, rearranging himself on the large branch where they were sitting. "How can you expect to see anything in *this* light? It may be true that we ourselves have not a clue where this count's hideout is, but I know for sure our good inspector isn't even looking in the right part of the valley."

"They could spend for ever just searching," said Scratch. "Unless Vermyn were to guide them there, of course." Both men twitched with laughter at the thought. It was nice to have an optional plan. It made them feel important.

"I'm cold and I'm bored," said Scratch, a little while later.

"You always are, unless you're eating something," said Itch. He nudged Scratch in the ribs. "Do you want to hear a joke?"

"Will it make me warmer?" asked Scratch.

"It might make you less bored."

"Go on then," said Scratch, who had never really cared for his brother's jokes.

"OK then. What do you call a German barber?"

"I don't know, brother, what do you call a German barber?"

"Herr Dresser!"

Itch nearly fell from the tree laughing at his

own joke. Scratch waited till he had calmed down before repeating, "I'm cold and I'm bored . . . *and* I'm not amused."

As the sun began to break on the horizon, and the steely light of dawn filtered into the sky, an exhausted Inspector Klaw yawned, and signalled to his men. "That's enough for tonight, boys," he told them wearily. "It's like looking for silver in a gold mine. Thank you all for your assistance."

Professor von Morcumstein had spent the hours in a carriage on the road above the valley, waiting for news. Now he could spy the inspector returning, he quickly climbed down from the carriage and trotted over to him.

"Well?" asked the professor. The inspector's expression revealed little sign of anything but tiredness.

"Not a thing. Sorry," he told the professor, shaking his head. "We could be searching for weeks and still not get anywhere."

"Hmm. In that case, we must encourage the count to come to us."

Klaw perked up. "Is that possible?"

"If the bait is right, I would say it is very possible."

"What sort of bait are we talking about?"

The professor grinned and said, "Could we find someone who does a good impersonation of a vampire?"

Their feet, soon to be followed by every part of their body, were quickly turning to stone.

◆ Chapter Six
What's the Matter with Walter?

The headline in the *Gertcha Gazette* the follow-ing morning read:

VAMPIRE COUNT SEIZED BY POLICE

Klaw and Professor von Morcumstein watched while the chief inspector of Gertcha gazed dubi-ously down at the article. "I hope you and the professor know what you're doing," he grumbled.

"The professor thought it would anger the real count," explained Klaw. "Apparently these vampire chaps have big egos. Therefore he may come out of hiding and reveal himself if he gets to hear that someone is claiming they are Count Arnold Krinkelfiend."

"Yes, well, I hope you're right," muttered the chief inspector. "This sort of thing scares the public, you know. Can lead to rioting."

Klaw didn't add that they had found an actor to pose as the count for pictures in the later edition of the *Gazette*, and that he was being kept in one of the cells in great comfort and at even greater expense.

The count was not in a good mood. He had had an argumentative evening with his son, Rupert, who had now left. And now Vermyn had hand delivered a copy of the *Gertcha Gazette* just before daybreak. The count angrily tossed it on the floor. "The impostor will die for this," he told Vermyn, and his voice bounced eerily off the earthen walls. "How dare this creature claim to be Count Arnold Krinkelfiend. There is only one Count Arnold Krinkelfiend, AND I AM HE."

"Er, yes, I was thinking it might prove of some interest to you, Your Countship," grinned Vermyn. He hoped it might be of enough interest to encourage another reward, but money was the last thing on the count's mind at that moment. The *first* thing on his mind was how he would go about dealing with the impostor.

As he paced the room, the thought of this "impostor" taking his place, suddenly gave the count a brilliant idea. He snapped his fingers in joy. It was all so simple. Why hadn't he thought of it earlier?

"Vermyn," smirked the count. "The king's head servant, Walter – our *accidental* hostage from the royal household – has suddenly become immensely useful."

"I am so genuinely glad to hear it, Your Countship," said Vermyn, and he *was* genuinely delighted, as he knew the count to be a generous man when in a good mood.

"I have a devilishly cunning plan which will make taking Viktoria Palace and proclaiming myself king easier than, say, stretching out my hand and strangling you without moving from this spot."

Vermyn began massaging his neck, imagining the count's strong bony fingers clasped around it. "Oh, er, wonderful, Your Countship. Yes, yes. Quite wonderful, indeed."

"Yes, Vermyn," said the count, turning to stare at his minion. "You have earned yourself a pay rise."

Vermyn grinned what would possibly be the biggest grin of his entire life.

King Konstantine and his daughter had just sat down to dinner when their head servant, Walter, walked in.

"Wa-Wa-Wa-" stuttered the king.

"Walter!" gasped the princess. "You have been freed!"

"Yes, Ma'am," said Walter.

The princess thought he was perhaps a bit thinner and paler than before, but other than that, he appeared remarkably well. "This is wonderful," she said. "We must tell all the staff, Papa."

"Er, should we?" said the king.

"Certainly. They have been so worried about you, dear Walter," smiled the princess.

"That is most gratifying, Ma'am. I will, in due course, get around to seeing them all individually. Firstly, with the king's kind permission, I would like to make an announcement to the household collectively. Could everyone be asked to gather in the ballroom please, Your Majesty?"

"Er, well . . . I suppose. . ."

"Of course they must, Papa," urged the princess. "Then we can hear all about Walter's adventures."

"Well, I'm keen to know about vampires," said the king. "See any of them while you were held hostage, Walter?"

Walter didn't reply; he merely shuddered.

"Let us finish our dinner, Walter, then we shall all assemble in the ballroom to hear the full story of your most unpleasant ordeal," the princess assured him.

"Yes. Most unpleasant business, I'm sure," said the king.

"Quite so, Your Majesty."

Walter bowed and left the room.

"After we have heard Walter's story, Papa, we must telephone Inspector Klaw," said the princess. "He will be overjoyed to learn of Walter's safe return."

"Will he? Yes, I suppose he will. Overjoyed," muttered the king. "That's the word. Overjoyed." The king sighed. "At least no one's going to try and take control of my palace. Couldn't have been doing with all of that."

The king's summons went quickly through the palace. A short time after the dinner things had been cleared away, everyone from the lowest to the highest was gathered in the ballroom.

The king untangled his feet from his beard and made a brief announcement. "Er, Walter, is, er, thankfully safely back with us. And, er, he has something, er, to say."

There was a short burst of applause as the king joined his thirty employees and Walter took his place on the podium.

An unpleasant grin began to stretch across the butler's face. Then he raised his arms and began to chant in an ancient tongue. Most present assumed it was a strange sort of poem: in fact, it was a spell.

As he spoke, everyone in the grand ballroom, without exception, found their legs would not move from where they were standing. Worse still, their feet, soon followed by every part of their body and all their clothes, were quickly turning to a grey-coloured stone.

"We've been deceived, Papa!" cried the princess in a desperate voice. As if to confirm her words, the man whom they thought to be Walter disintgrated before their eyes. His face elongated and his skin became even paler, bloodless – almost translucent. His hands lengthened, becoming bony and claw-like. As Walter's familiar features rapidly became unrecognizable, a tall figure in a top hat emerged.

The count laughed an evil, victorious laugh. "I have done it, thanks to my cloaking skills," he boasted. "I have taken the palace. I am now king."

The king, the princess and all the employees could say or do nothing in response.

Inspector Klaw and Professor von Morcumstein had waited all day and much of the night, thinking the count might make an appearance on learning about their "prisoner". As the time passed, they had to conclude sadly that the fake vampire plan had failed.

But Klaw had also been working on another plan. He felt certain that if the count was a vampire, others had to be involved – minions from the daylight world who would run errands and keep the count well informed. Klaw had gone through his criminal record books and come up with several possible names. Only two of them lived in Grund. Klaw pencilled them into his notebook. "The Ripaka Brothers," he whispered. "Also known as Itch and Scratch."

Itch and Scratch were happily enjoying their favourite pastime – eating anything that passed as food, and some things that probably didn't, but were worth eating anyway – when a net fell from a tree above and entangled them.

"HELP!" shouted Scratch.

"WATCH OUT FOR MY SANDWICH!" shouted

Itch, as the net tightened around them. Then several Grund police officers leapt from their hiding places in the tree, and dragged Itch and Scratch to a horse and cart, where they underwent a short ride to the police station.

The count looked into the hall mirror. A bit pointless, really, because he had no reflection.

Chapter Seven

A King Without a Conscience

ount Arnold Krinkelfiend, self-proclaimed King of Gertcha, was enjoying a night of celebration. The king, he found, kept a well-supplied drinks cabinet. A few glasses of port added to the fun of standing in front of his newly acquired stone statues, singing ancient songs.

He looked with dignity into a hall mirror, while straightening his hair. A bit pointless, really, because – being a vampire – he had no reflection.

"Today, Gertcha, tomorrow . . . tomorrow, other places," he shouted to no one in particular. Taking the palace and making himself king had been easy with a bit of cloaking magic. But he was cross with himself for not having thought of it the moment Vermyn had brought him the king's head servant. However, being king was a trifle compared with the true reason why he had so badly wanted control of the palace: the secret it held that surely no one alive could possibly know about unless he were of vampire stock (and if of vampire stock, he wouldn't, strictly speaking, *be* alive). It would take him a little time to find it – this near-mythical gem he was searching for. So far it was no more than an illustration in an ancient book. But once he had his hands on the real, magical object, he would be the most powerful force the earth had ever witnessed.

The count glanced through a window and noticed that morning was about to break. "Time to take a rest," he muttered. "Oh, how I wish I had my favourite coffin, or, at the very least, my cupboard at Windfall Castle. This sofa –" he winced at the word – "is impossible to get comfortable on." He rubbed his bony hands together. "No matter," he grinned. "I just have one more little job to do and then I can relax."

He picked up the telephone and called the *Gertcha Gazette*.

The morning headline made shocking reading:

GERTCHA HAS NEW KING

KING KRINKELFIEND, FORMERLY COUNT ARNOLD OF WINDFALL CASTLE, TAKES CONTROL AT VIKTORIA PALACE.

The article stunned the citizens and governing council of Grund. *King Konstantine dethroned . . .* the article went on. *New king to make sweeping changes to life in Gertcha. . . New king to declare war on Gotcha and other mid-European countries. . . Palace household put in permanent sleep . . .* and so on.

The law was helpless to intervene. The count had outmanoeuvred them. Not only was he king, but it seemed that anyone who tried to question it would be turned to stone.

Klaw screwed the paper into a ball and tossed it over his shoulder. The count had moved so much faster than they had imagined he would.

"I feel so very bad about all of this," apologized Professor von Morcumstein, who was sitting opposite the inspector in his office.

"Hardly your fault, Professor," said Klaw. "It was me who dragged you away from the university. You weren't supposed to be here on a vampire hunt. And anyway," he sighed, "I've made a little progress with the Ripaka brothers – Itch and Scratch. It seems they are two of the count's spies."

This was quite true. The brothers had, after some negotiation, told the inspector about Vermyn, and that Vermyn could lead them to the count's lair. Although reaching the lair was a bit late to be of much use in apprehending the count himself, with any luck it would lead them to Walter and Ivor Brandt.

The Windfall Castle clock struck midnight. Rupert Krinkelfiend, accepting that his mad and dangerous father was not there, turned himself into a bat and took to the air. He had left his father's lair in Silver Valley in a bit of a huff following their argument, and returned to his own castle to ponder his next move. But the news that reached him there had been too alarming for him to stand back and ponder any longer. Viktoria Palace, of all places. What did his father want with a palace? He never had liked palaces. But the gardener, Max, bore out the stories in the newspapers; according to him, the count really did want to be king and rule from Viktoria Palace.

As Rupert winged a steady course towards the palace, Inspector Klaw was making a less than steady descent through the undergrowth of Silver Valley. In one hand he held a long wooden stake. The other hand, thanks to Itch and Scratch, was attached to Vermyn.

Itch and Scratch had led Klaw to Vermyn's secret den in Fortune Forest earlier that day. Klaw, accompanied by two officers, had burst in upon Vermyn, knocking over a small table where he'd been counting out his kronks. There was a bit of a kerfuffle but Vermyn was outnumbered, and the inspector soon had his man. They dragged him out of the thick of the forest to a waiting police cart.

Vermyn gave the inspector the exact location of the count's lair, and that night the inspector found himself back in sinister Silver Valley. But this time he found what he was looking for. When he saw the door at the base of a great oak tree slide back, he understood how impossible it would have been to find the vampire's lair without inside help.

Two officers waited on the outside, keeping guard. Vermyn led the inspector ever-downwards through the underground maze.

"Well I never," gasped the inspector, with a mixture of shock and admiration, as the flaming torches magically ignited themselves to light their gentle descent.

"This is a mere sideshow compared to what you will witness should you come face to face with the count," warned Vermyn through a grin.

"You can be quiet," Klaw told him, and yanked on his handcuffs just to show him who was in charge of whom.

They soon found Brandt and Walter locked in a

cage suspended from the ceiling. Brandt was as well as he ever was, though noticeably smellier. He smiled and waved and asked if they had any sand-wiches with them.

Walter was not in such a good state. For a start, he had been turned to stone.

"What happened?" Klaw asked Brandt, as he cut through the padlock on the cage door with a pair of boltcutters.

"Don't think the count took much of a liking to Walter," said Brandt. "Mind you, he didn't take much of a liking to me, either."

"Then why weren't you turned to stone, too?"

"Ah well, you see, the count did try, but his stone-turning spell just wouldn't work on me. I told him I must have some natural ability to repulse his magic. And he agreed – he said something about me being totally repulsive."

Klaw opened the cage door and pulled Brandt clear.

"Now what are you going to do with that?" sneered Vermyn, gesturing at the statue of Walter with a grin.

Klaw grinned back at him. "The three of us are

going to carry our statuesque friend out into the open: you and me at one end, Mr Brandt at the other."

Once outside, the two officers assisted, but it was a long and tiresome effort heaving the statue up the hillside and over the ridge of the valley.

"Well done, everyone," sighed the inspector. "You can all go back to town now." He blew a whistle, and a couple of police carriages rattled into sight. "You'd better get home to your wife and family," he said to Brandt. "Your wife's been very worried about you."

"Right you are," smiled the simple woodcutter, who looked none the worse for his escapade. "I hope she's got something cooking. I'm famished."

"Welcome, my former son," smiled Arnold Krinkelfiend as Rupert Krinkelfiend entered the great hall and changed from bat to human form in one easy motion. "Welcome to King Arnold Palace," he continued.

"Good evening, Father," said Rupert. "And how did you sleep in your new abode?"

"Like the dead; which isn't bad considering I had to rough it. They haven't a coffin in the house."

Rupert followed his father into a spacious wood-panelled study, where each of the four walls held row upon row of leather-bound books. "A glass of something to chill the blood?" offered his father.

"Not right now, thank you. I never drink when I'm flying."

"Of course, I forgot how sensible you always were," mocked his father. "So, you have re-considered my offer? You have come to join me in my work?"

"I've come to see what, exactly, you are up to," replied Rupert. "I see I find you in a particularly cheerful mood this evening."

The count smiled and poured himself a generous measure of vintage port. "Let us just say that I have found what I am looking for."

"Perhaps so, but you were never interested in owning a palace, so why is it—"

"Oh, my dear Rupert. Can it be that you are really so stupid? This pile of rubble can roll down the hill-top, for all I care," spat the count, alarming his son.

"It is not the palace that interests me."

The count regained his composure and raised his glass. "A toast. A toast to me – King Krinkelfiend."

Rupert waited while his father drained his glass. "Then what is it you're interested in?" he asked.

The count gently put down his glass, and looked directly into Rupert's eyes. "Come, my former son. I wish to show you something which, despite being half human, will, I feel sure, fascinate you."

He led Rupert across the room to a table, upon which lay an open book. The page displayed a painting of Dracula's dagger.

"Very pretty," remarked Rupert.

"Yes, pretty – and infinitely powerful," said the count. "I have spent many years in search of it. And now. . ."

He left the sentence unfinished and wiped away an imagined tear that he could feel trickling down his porcelain cheek. He gently closed the book.

"Look, Father," said Rupert, desperate to discuss the reason for his visit. "I've been reading about your antics in the paper."

"What antics? You knew already that I had taken

over the palace," shrugged his father.

"It's not the palace I mean," he told him. "It's the inhabitants of the palace. The papers say you have turned them all to stone."

"Ah, my caring, all-too-human son," grimaced Krinkelfiend. "They are fortunate I did not destroy them, instead. They are still alive – they just don't get around so much any more."

"Father, this is despicable behaviour. You have no right—"

"NO RIGHT?" bellowed his father. "I have every right. I am on the verge of becoming the most powerful force on the planet."

Rupert was about to complain of his father's cruelty, when it suddenly became clear to him. He pointed to the book on the table.

"You – you've found it here, haven't you?" Rupert said, aghast. "You've found Dracula's dagger."

Count Arnold Krinkelfiend released a mad laugh. "Oh yes, indeed. I have found the dagger of our Master. Now I will be his chosen one."

Rupert said no more on the matter, but he was thinking hard about his next move. "Grund must

have a police station," he said to himself. "I
think it's time I began some work of my own."

It was morning by the time Klaw, the police chief
and the professor gathered at the police station to
examine the statue more closely.

"So, unless we get the count to help us – which is
virtually impossible – our friend here will remain a
stone statue for all time?" remarked a bewildered
chief, as he tried to clarify the situation.

"That is how it appears to be," nodded the
professor, but his concern for the ex-king's ex-head
servant was outweighed by his fascination. "This
vampire is quite the most wonderful technician.
Notice the texture of the stone. It is perfect, and all
from one spell. Place it in a public garden and attach
a fountain, and it would not appear the remotest bit
out of place."

"When we've finished congratulating Count
Arnold Krinkelfiend on turning a citizen of this
town into a potential park fountain," said the chief,
with heavy sarcasm, "can we turn our attention to
our problems, gentlemen?"

Klaw looked to the professor. "Well," sighed the great academic, "unless we can gain the sympathy of the count, I'm afraid it won't just be our friend here who will be experiencing life as a statue."

"I think we should go back to my apartment and start working on a plan," said the inspector.

"Good idea," nodded the professor.

"Yes, a great idea," said the chief. "For a start, it gets you out from under my feet. But don't take too long in coming up with something, Klaw. We don't know what this mad count has planned for us."

*Klaw found himself blankly shaking hands
with a young man who was clearly a vampire.*

✣ Chapter Eight
Krinkelfiend Befriends the Law

Inspector Klaw and Professor von Morcumstein spent several hours discussing ideas on what they should do to save the palace from the count. Klaw even considered calling in the army to carry out a full attack on the palace. But the professor pointed out that they would probably all be turned into statues like Walter. So, they decided to go to bed and discuss it again first thing in the morning.

(The professor had been staying in Inspector Klaw's spare bedroom as his guest. The inspector felt it was the least he could do, considering it was he who prevented the professor from returning to his home town, some days ago.)

Inspector Klaw had only been in bed a few moments when he saw the strangest sight he had ever seen – there was a bat on his bedroom window ledge knocking with its wing to be let in!

With slight hesitation, Klaw opened the window and the bat flew in. After circling the room a moment, the bat exploded in a cloud of purple smoke. Moments later, Klaw found himself blankly shaking hands with a young man in a cloak who was clearly a vampire – or so past conversations with the professor would have led him to believe.

"I'm sorry about the hour," apologized the visitor, in a very gentlemanly fashion. "I know you humans tend to do your sleeping during the night. I've always envied you that. How I would love to watch the sunrise; see rays of light sparkle on ocean waters."

"Er. . ." said Klaw, though part of him was hoping

he was still asleep and dreaming. "Can I get you anything?"

"No thanks. I never drink when I'm flying," replied Rupert. "By the way, I followed you here when you left your office. That is how I discovered where you live."

"I see," blinked Klaw, not seeing anything much at all.

The bedroom door creaked open. Both of them turned to see Professor von Morcumstein filling the entrance, in his nightgown and nightcap.

"I heard voices." He stared excitedly at the visitor. "You are Count Arnold Krinkelfiend!" he stated, rather than asked.

"Er, no," replied the young man, "I'm his son, Rupert, and I need your help."

"Your family is of vampire descent?" the professor urged.

"Er, yes, I suppose it is, really."

"*Mein Gott!* If it is so, then you are the first truly genuine vampire I have met in some fifty years of study. I cannot tell you what joy this moment brings to me."

They moved into the sitting room, where Rupert explained what had been happening at Viktoria Palace.

"I can free the spell that the household is under," he told them, "but I need a distraction. If my father thought I had joined the 'enemy', he would turn me to stone without a moment's hesitation. He has already disowned me because I demonstrate too many human traits. My mother, you see, was human."

Klaw looked at the professor then back to the young Krinkelfiend. "How do we know we can trust you?" he asked.

Rupert frowned. It hurt him that they could doubt his good intentions. "You have my word that it is not a trap. However, if you have a better plan. . .?" He deliberately left the sentence unfinished.

The professor raised a finger. "You mentioned we should distract your father. What do you propose, exactly?"

"Perhaps a diversion of some kind on one of the upper floors of the palace, while I enter the ballroom on the ground floor and free everyone."

"It would be possible, I imagine," nodded Klaw.

"There is one little thing I should mention," said Rupert, and he turned to the professor, because he knew he would understand. "I'm afraid my father has discovered Dracula's dagger."

The professor sharply drew breath. *"Mein Gott!"* he gasped, for the second time.

"Is that important in our investigation?" the inspector innocently enquired.

The professor rested a hand on the policeman's shoulder. "This near mythical dagger," explained the professor, "has powers way beyond your or my imaginations, Inspector. If someone could learn how to tap into its powers, they would become all-powerful – utterly invincible."

"This gets better and better," groaned Klaw, rubbing his tired eyes.

"I think I should also mention," added Rupert, "that I cannot, and would not, attempt to kill my father. His powers, even without the dagger, are amazing. And, whatever he has done and intends to do, he is still my father."

"I can understand your loyalty," said the inspector.

"All I can do is delay him with moderate spells."

"That might be enough," said the professor. "The dagger is our main concern. If we could get our hands on it, we might not only save the occupants of the palace, but all of mankind."

It was a sobering thought. Inspector Klaw stood up and shook the vampire by the hand. "I admire you for coming here tonight. We will do everything in our power to help you to reach a successful end to this nightmare."

"Thank you," smiled Rupert. "Thank you very much. Now all we need do is work out the finer details."

It was dark and moonless outside the palace walls. "Wait here," said Rupert to the inspector and the professor. "I'll take a little look around first."

"*Mein Gott!*" gasped the professor, as Rupert exploded into a bat. "He can transmogrify *and* he can fly! This is quite exceptional, my dear Inspector. I am totally overwhelmed."

Rupert soon returned, and changed back into his human form. "There's definitely an air vent up there. Just a question of getting up this wall."

Before the other two could ask how he intended scaling the wall, he had clicked his fingers, said a few words and there was a ladder.

"Let's go."

As they followed Rupert up the ladder, the professor mumbled something about devoting his remaining years to rewriting his works on vampire behaviour and magic.

The descent into the dark ballroom was not as drastic as the professor had nervously been anticipating. Several times he'd pointed out he was too old for this sort of exercise, but with a little further help from their vampire friend – in the form of another ladder – they were safely inside.

And once inside, Klaw and the professor saw how serious the problem was.

"Sentenced to sleep for ever," whispered the inspector in a detached voice, as they gazed upon rows of stone figures.

"*Mein Gott!*" gasped the professor, yet again. "This one is King Konstantine of Gertcha."

"I'm terribly sorry about all this," said Rupert,

pulling a small notepad from his pocket. "I'll just check my spell book, then I can get to work on reviving them all. I think now might be the time you go looking for Father. He'll need distracting while I work on a spell."

"You hope to distract *me*?" mocked a deep voice from somewhere quite near.

The three of them looked behind them, in front of them, and to the side.

"Up here!" called the voice.

Glancing up they now saw a large, red-eyed bat hanging from a chandelier. It dropped gracefully to the floor, at once becoming Count Krinkelfiend.

"What a very cunning threesome you make, I must say," smiled the count, but it wasn't a very warm smile. "As for you, my former son, you would have done better keeping your wings out of this."

"Before you go doing anything rash," persisted Rupert, "what real use are this palace and these people to you? You have found what you really came here for. Why not leave in peace?"

"Because for centuries we vampires have not been left in peace," snapped the count. "That is why, my former son. From the very beginning, we were seen as bloodsucking bats. What utter nonsense."

"It is accepted as a myth based upon your true history," said the professor, wishing he had the opportunity to sit down with the count and discuss vampire history. "Bat-like creatures, half man, half mammal, were sighted along the southern end of the Carpathian mountains. You, yourself, were first sighted in Moldavia, I believe."

The count bowed and took a step nearer the professor. "Quite so, my learned friend," he said. "And you agree with me, Professor von Morcumstein – oh yes, it is my business to know who you are – that the vampire is a threatened species?"

"Perhaps once, but no one has persecuted a vampire in recent decades," said the professor.

"That is all *you* know," shouted the count. "Anyway, enough of this talk. I have the dagger, and that is all that matters." The count's eyes glazed over as he thought of the beautiful, beloved dagger. "Marvin, the blind monk, must have been remarkable to have created such beauty combined with such power."

"Marvin?" gasped the professor. "Marvin, who is supposed to still haunt the University of Grund? Now it all fits together. His mysterious death all those years ago *is* linked to the dagger."

"How he died has nothing to do with the dagger," said the count. "Marvin ended up in a vat of wine. That is all."

"Perhaps Dracula saw him as a threat?" suggested the professor.

"No one is a threat to the mighty Dracula, Professor," said the count. "You would do well to remember that."

After a lengthy, and silent, pause, Inspector Klaw coughed nervously. "Excuse me for changing the subject, but can't you at least free these sleeping people and turn Walter back into a human being? He takes up a lot of office space, and he scares my secretary."

"Of course I can," nodded the count. "But I won't. Now, have you any more questions? I am very busy."

"Yes, many," said the professor. "How did the dagger come to be brought here?"

"It was brought here during a time of uprising between the Gots and Gerts," replied the count.

"That would make sense," said the professor. "The palace would have been better fortified than most other places."

The count nodded. "A long-ago vampire family, concerned for their personal safety, thought the palace – as the professor rightly points out – better protected than all other available alternatives. The intention, I imagine, was to hide the dagger and return at a later date to collect their most priceless item. But amidst the chaos which ensued there were naturally more pressing considerations. Alas, the future was cruel to them. They had to travel far away, and became separated from the dagger for ever." He tapped his chest rather grandly. "When taking over this palace, I tried to picture what I would have done with such an object. Even the most deeply hidden item usually surfaces at one time or other, often as not by pure chance. Then it came to me." He glanced at the professor, pleased to see him hanging on every word. "If a man has stolen a walking stick, the best place to hide it is among people with walking sticks."

"In other words," said the professor, "the best way to hide something is *not* to hide it at all." Professor von Morcumstein sighed and shook his head as all became clear. "Naturally, therefore," he said, "the best way to hide a dagger is to display it with other daggers and weapons and artefacts. So you found the dagger among one of the numerous collections of knives, swords and daggers within the palace?"

"Right again, Herr Professor. Are you quite sure you are not a vampire yourself?'"

Rupert, who had been looking for an opportunity to do something useful, decided to act while his father's attention was focused on the professor. He burst into his bat form and launched himself upon his father's neck. It was, sadly, a futile attempt to get the better of him: a last ditch effort to gain the upper hand.

The count side-stepped the oncoming bat, clicked his fingers once, and watched – as they all did – the bat freeze in mid-air, defying all the laws of gravity.

"Incredible," tutted the professor, examining the motionless bat, like it was some great work of art in a gallery.

"A mere party trick," the count responded modestly. "But thank you all the same." He rested a conspiratorial hand upon the professor's shoulder. "In another time and place, I would have much enjoyed sharing a longer acquaintance with you, Herr Professor. Alas. . ." Then he closed his eyes and began chanting one of his numerous spells.

With that, Professor von Morcumstein and Inspector Klaw were turned into solid stone statues.

Count Krinkelfiend changed into a bat and flew
through the nearest window.

✦ Chapter Nine
Dagger on the Loose

Victory is a strange thing. The challenge is so often more rewarding than achievement of the ultimate goal. This was what the count was contemplating in the silence that followed his exit from the ballroom. There was nothing standing in his way to complete power.

But as the count was making his way to the pantry to see if there was anything fresh to eat in the mousetraps, his son was proving to own greater powers than those with which he had been credited. Inside the dark ballroom his bat form began to glow purple. With a mighty effort he burst forth as a ball of flame before reappearing as his true self.

"That worked out a bit better than I'd anticipated," he thought aloud, brushing himself down with the back of his hand. "If Father *had* turned me to stone, we really would have been in trouble." He took a deep breath. "Now to go and sort him out!"

Pausing at the door he whispered back to his motionless companions, "I'll be back in a minute, all being well. Don't go away!"

Count Arnold had picked up the limp mice he'd found, and was moving back into the kitchen to find two slices of bread to put them between. "Nothing tastes as good as a meal you've prepared yourself," he muttered, then he noticed he had company.

"So there you are, Father," said Rupert. "Surely, you didn't think a statue-making spell would trouble me for long?"

"Back annoying me so soon?" sneered the count.

"You've behaved very badly. I can't allow it to continue," Rupert told him.

"Do not patronize me," spat the count, venomously. "I gave you existence; taught you the vampire way. Your shows of human weakness have shamed you and, frankly, disappointed me. When your mother passed away, you chose to live alone, not wishing to rest under my roof. So be it. But, just to make sure you do not continue to interfere, it is for your own good, my boy, that I now must atomize you and reassemble you as a four-headed dog. At least I shall always have a head to pat, and I'll be able to keep you on a leash at my side at all times. And *that* is a spell you will not shake off quite so easily."

Before the count could raise a dangerous finger in anger, his son darted from the room, cape flapping behind him. He knew he could not out-magic his father in a face-to-face confrontation, but it was possible he could outsmart him. And on that he was depending.

"I know this palace better than you!" shouted his father, sprinting after him in hot pursuit. "There is nowhere you can hide where I cannot find you."

Count Krinkelfiend raced into the main hallway. "I'll find you eventually," he threatened, his booming voice bouncing off the high ceilings and walls. "It's only a question of time. And when I do find you. . ." He left the sentence unfinished. He thought it sounded scarier that way.

The count was not in the best of physical conditions. Huffing and puffing, he sat down on one of the hallway chairs for a rest.

"Ouch!" squealed the chair.

"How very strange," he muttered. "How is it that a chair can say, 'Ouch!'?"

He put his head between his legs and examined the chair. "It looks like an ordinary chair," he thought.

"Excuse me!" said the chair, darting away down an adjoining corridor, leaving the count sprawled on his backside.

"So, you have mastered the art of cloaking," growled the count, angrily. "I will show you how to cloak properly, you amateur."

His son didn't intend sticking around long enough to find out. He stopped being a chair and sprinted headlong into one of the bedrooms.

The bedroom door burst open. "Aha!" said his father, raising his long arms. "Now I have you cornered. You nearly lost me for a moment. However, nearly is not enough."

As his father rambled on, Rupert backed away, stumbling against a table. "It's no good trying to escape again," warned his father. "It's the leash and collar for you, my boy. But have no fear. I'll feed you twice daily and take you for walks every night."

Rupert grabbed at the first solid object he could find on the table. The count at once backed off. "Put that away, dear boy," he told Rupert, and his voice was suddenly gentle, almost soothing in tone. Rupert, who was confused by the abrupt change in his father, glanced at the object he had picked up. The dagger in his hand glistened in the candlelight of the room.

Rupert grinned and began to stroke the dagger gently. "Well, well, Father," he said. "A bit careless not putting it away somewhere very safe, wouldn't you say?"

"But it is of no use to you," said the count, who seemed to have shrunk in size and no longer looked remotely invincible.

Rupert backed towards a window. "It seems a shame to throw the dagger away, but then. . ."

"I'll share its powers, just don't damage it," begged his father.

Rupert smiled. "I think I will just keep it awhile," he said. "It might be useful in undoing the spell you put on those people in the ballroom."

"Yes, yes," said Count Krinkelfiend. "The ballroom. Let's go there now and free everyone. Then you can give me back the dagger. A fair deal?"

Rupert knew it wasn't wise to trust his father, but it was possibly his only hope of helping the others. "Perhaps, Father, but you lead the way. I'll follow a few paces behind, I think."

"Of course, my boy," smiled the count.

Once back in the ballroom, Count Krinkelfield clicked his fingers. Everyone slowly began to return to their normal selves. They were stiff and tired, as if waking from a great sleep. Not that anyone knew it at that moment, but at Grund police station, Walter was returning to normal, too.

"I've kept my side of the bargain. Now give me the dagger," said the count.

An immense ray of green light tore out of the biggest of its Burmese rubies, and it became unbearably cold to hold. Rupert at once dropped it.

"You see," laughed the count. "It doesn't want you to hold it." And with that, Count Krinkelfiend rapidly changed into a bat, pounced upon the dagger and flew through the nearest window and out into the dark night, leaving an explosion of shattered glass in his wake.

"Oh no!" cried Rupert, falling to the floor and searching among everyone's feet. "He's escaped, and he's taken the dagger!"

"So I see," said Klaw, examining the million fragments of glass all over the ballroom floor. "Where's he likely to go?"

Rupert shrugged desperately. "Impossible to know."

"I very much doubt he'll return to his hideout in Silver Valley," mused the professor. "He will assume we know where it is. His safest bet would be to go high up, where it is difficult to follow him on foot."

"Does he have new powers from this dagger?" asked Klaw.

"Not yet," said Rupert, "But he is no fool – *and* he seems to understand the dagger. It is only a matter of time."

King Konstantine and Princess Lashka approached Klaw. "My dear Inspector, what on earth's been going on?" demanded the king. "And who broke my window?"

"Father," said Princess Lashka, "this is no time to be worrying about a broken window. We must thank the inspector for saving our lives."

"It is Rupert Krinkelfiend you must thank, Your Highness," said Inspector Klaw.

Princess Lashka's eyes met Rupert's, and they both smiled at each other.

"You have performed miracles," the princess told him.

"And who's been helping themselves to my vintage port?" continued the king, as he moved towards his drinks cabinet.

"It was, er. . . It was nothing, Princess Lashka," said Rupert, gracefully bowing his head.

"Unfortunately, Your Royal Highnesses, our troubles are far from over," said the professor. "The count has taken a most powerful secret weapon away from your palace. He must be stopped."

"And if he is not?" she asked.

"Then it is possible he will become the most powerful force on the whole of our planet."

🦇　🦇🦇　🦇

The professor, with his uncanny awareness of vampire behaviour, had accurately predicted the count's next move. He was at that very moment flying beyond the hills and valleys, ever higher, towards the Tryfoolian mountain range, some sixty miles from Grund, as the bat flies.

The air was cold enough to freeze a mortal to death, but the count felt nothing despite the thin layer of snow forming across his thin blue lips and wing tips. The dagger was clasped in his hooked, furry claws.

A dull metal glow on the horizon, announcing the onslaught of daybreak, spread like a disease across the sky. "Faster, faster!" the count urged himself.

A mountain shepherd driving cattle to fresh pasture on a lower slope stared blankly up as the dark form of the count shot overhead and disappeared into a pine forest.

"Must be the strangest owl I've ever seen," said the shepherd.

The count landed in the snow, transforming back into human form as he did so. He sniggered as he pulled out the dagger from a pocket and removed its glistening sheath. Glancing about him, he saw he'd found sanctuary in a pine forest, and a short inspection of the terrain brought him to a tiny cavern within some rocks. It was comfortable enough, and, more importantly, shut out the daylight. He could rest there until darkness fell.

Back at the palace, someone opened the curtains to let in the first of the morning light. It was a natural enough thing to have done – unless you happened to have a vampire in the room.

Strictly speaking, Rupert should have disintegrated into a pile of ashes then and there. But he was so preoccupied with the severity of the situation that for the first time in his life he hadn't even noticed the daylight. It was the professor who gasped, "The curse of the daylight!"

With a sharp intake of breath, Rupert threw both

arms up to his eyes. It was a gesture, if a worthless one, intended to shield him from the sun's vampire-killing rays.

But nothing happened.

The professor clapped his hands excitedly. "It can mean only one thing," he told him. "You are not a vampire! At least, not in the true sense of the term. It would seem you have inherited more of your mother's genes than your father's."

"Then I am mostly human?"

"Precisely so," nodded the professor.

It was all becoming clear in Rupert's mind. "Because I was educated in the magic ways of the vampire, it was assumed that I *was* a vampire."

The happiest of smiles appeared on Rupert's lips as the good news sunk in. "This means I can walk in the streets; lie in the sunshine; complain when the weather is too warm. I can live the life so far denied me. I can lead a *normal* life," he sighed happily.

"All this I imagine to be true, my friend," nodded the professor. Then he added, "Welcome to the land of the living."

With a deafening scream, the count cast a spell
that would blast his son off the face of the mountain.

❧ Chapter Ten
The Final Confrontation

Rupert knew it was down to him to stop his father. He was about to take to the air, when the professor rushed to him and whispered in his ear. The young man nodded thoughtfully, then he was gone, heading for the Tryfoolian mountain range.

As Rupert approached the region where the count was hiding, all the count's senses told him his son was in the vicinity, yet he could not understand how it was possible. "He cannot be out in daylight!" he repeated numerous times to himself. "He would die in daylight!" But he could hardly go outside and investigate, so he remained sheltered and waited to see what would unfold. He continued to caress the dagger. The dagger would protect him, for the dagger knew how much he adored it.

Rupert changed into human form and landed gently in the snow. What made it a particularly soft landing was the flattened shepherd underneath him. "Thank you," he smiled, brushing the snow from the old man's coat. "Most considerate of you."

"What is all this?" gasped the old man, his breath freezing on the icy wind. "First a strange-looking owl, and now a man flying through the air!"

"You say you saw a strange owl?" cried Rupert, clasping the man's lapels.

"That's right. Just up yonder in the pines. It crash-landed there. And if there's any more of this, I'm putting in a formal complaint. We don't need creatures crashing out of the sky and scaring the animals and. . ."

Rupert slipped away, leaving the poor shepherd nattering away to himself. Once in the pines, he needed no special senses to track his father: he followed the footprints in the virgin snow that led forever upwards.

Inside his shelter, the count was suddenly aware that the dagger was growing warmer. Not too warm, but pleasantly warm. The dagger seemed to have a mind of its own. It had been cold at the palace, and was warm now.

"What can it mean?" wondered the count. "Is the spirit of Dracula stirring within it?" Then it glowed silver, and the big Burmese ruby in its hilt glazed over, milky at first, as it became mirror-like. From within the depths of this mirror a miniature face appeared. Could he be staring into the illustrious features of the infamous Count Dracula? The dagger had belonged to Dracula – contained his spirit, or so it was written.

"Go out into the open!" came a whispered instruction from the tiny image. The count was delighted. At last, the dagger was communicating with him, and not just by changing its temperature.

"I cannot go out," he explained. "It is daylight."

"Trust the power. If you trust it, it will protect you and provide for you."

"I do trust it, I do trust it," stammered the count.

"Go out into the open!" reiterated the dagger, which, cooling, regained its normal form.

The count breathed deeply and clambered to his feet. With some trepidation he burrowed upwards and squeezed between the jagged rocks. He paused briefly on the threshold then surged out into daylight. "Trust the power, trust the power, trust the power!" he cried.

As his eyes adjusted to the harshness of a light he was unused to, he saw the black figure of his son hunched over some footprints in the snow.

"It is daylight, yet I live," boasted the count, shielding his pained eyes against that very daylight. He waved the dagger wildly above his head. "I have the power."

"And so do I," said his son. "I'm still in one piece, too, and unlike you, Father, I do not require props!"

"I do not know what sorcery permits you to move

in the daylight world, but in a moment you will cease to exist," the count replied.

As his father raised his arms to perform some ghastly spell, Rupert stood up and faced him.

"What if the dagger decides to favour *me*?" he asked. "I mean, just because you are holding it doesn't give you any special right over its power. Has it promised to obey you? Who is in control of whom?"

His father continued to hold his arms up, but his expression showed a glimmer of doubt. His son had a point. Seeing this doubt, Rupert quickly pushed home his advantage. "After all, I could say I trust its powers as much as you do. Words are only words."

"The dagger is mine and mine to command!" insisted his father. "I found it. I knew of its existence. Not you. It talks to me."

"Surely no one but Vlad Basarab himself has true control over such a thing?" said his son. "You *stole* the dagger. The dagger did not come to you through any desire of its own." Then Rupert chuckled. "How ironic," he said, "that we should be face to face with

Dracula's dagger in this bleak snow-covered region. You, of all people, will need little reminding that, on a winter's day in 1476, Vlad Dracula came to a bloody end in a snow-covered forest in the southeast of Transylvania."

The count had had enough. With a deafening scream, he cast a spell that would blast his son and anyone nearby off the face of the mountain. Nothing happened. A few sparks sizzled at the end of the dagger, but that was all.

"You see, Father! The dagger has drained you of your powers, *not* improved them," said Rupert, the calmness in his tone masking his quaking nerves. Although he trusted the professor, Rupert couldn't help the nagging doubt that perhaps this time he was wrong. He tossed his head at the sky. "The sun rises and you weaken. You will surely die."

"What has happened?" the count whimpered.

Rupert stepped closer to him, the snow crunching beneath his feet. "The professor told me something as I left to come here," he explained in a soft, almost kindly manner. "He suddenly remembered that Dracula's dagger was powerful because it fed on power. You see, it doesn't *give* power, it *takes* it. I imagine it tricked you into the daylight just so it could feed off your powers while you wilt away to nothing. Am I right?"

With fear in his eyes, the count put the dagger in its sheath and threw it as far as he could. But it was too late to reverse the situation. His skin began to shrivel away like the dead skin of a snake, and his body crumpled as age ravaged him.

"No, no, no!" he screamed, disappearing in a pool of melting snow. Rupert shuddered, and turned his head away. Though he had no great love or respect for his father, he couldn't bear witnessing the horror and pain before him. His mother had died suddenly when he was a boy, and now this. He suddenly felt very alone.

Soon all that remained of the count was a cape and top hat, and a deep hole where the snow around him had evaporated. His demise broke the many spells he had put upon people during his long lifetime. All those he had turned into statues over many, many years became people again. The poor creatures inside the cupboard at Castle Windfall burst out of their tiny cages and their wooden prison, unable to comprehend how they had become free human beings once more.

Suddenly, the ground began to rumble, signalling the beginning of an avalanche. Whether the dagger was the cause of it, or whether it was bizarre co-incidence, it appeared that Dracula's cast-away weapon was intended for permanent burial beneath a mountain of snow.

Rupert took to the air as pine trees snapped like matchsticks, and came hurtling down the mountain-side in a roaring, thunderous, swirling blur. The air was soon thick with gusting sprays of snow, and for a short time Rupert could see nothing in the freez-ing hell.

It was many minutes before he dared drop back down to the ground far below. Even then the wind continued to howl, and the snow continued to shift in small unequal sections.

When all was truly calm, he surveyed the horrible scenes of devastation. He was relieved to see the shepherd and his flock appearing safely from a barn in a lower field, unaffected by the catastrophe on high. As for his father, there was nothing left of him. And the dagger was in the best possible place – in a frozen grave, for ever out of the reach of mortal man and vampire.

With the grating sound of metal on metal, the long snaking line of silver coaches inched out of the railway station at Grund.

Inspector Klaw waved until the train was out of sight, and then returned to his office. He was both delighted and relieved all had worked out well. It was the most extraordinary yet most exciting case he had ever worked on.

Professor von Morcumstein sat back in his seat. In an hour he would go to the buffet car and have something to eat. In eight hours he would be at Cluj, the capital of Transylvania. There he would change trains and begin the long, long journey through Hungary, Czechoslovakia and Germany. It would be several days before he was back in his tiny home in Muhlhausen.

"Maybe it is time to retire from touring to concentrate on giving the world a definitive book on vampires," thought the professor, as he glanced out of the murky window upon the distant peaks of the mountains. "Somewhere out there is Count Dracula's dagger," he mused, and its loss to the world as a link to the history of the vampire made him unusually melancholy.

Yet, deep in his heart, the professor knew that a dagger with such unknown powers could not remain lost for ever. "Some day, it will reappear, and then it will show us all what it can really do. I only hope it is in my own lifetime."

Look out for the sequel to
Count Krinkelfiend's Quest:

The Return of the Count

Decomposing corpses risen from the grave, the disgruntled ghost of a fifteenth-century soldier, more bat-like apparitions … it can mean but one thing – more vampirish goings-on in Transylvania.

Never fear, Inspector Klaw, Professor von Morcumstein and Count Krinkelfiend's former son, Rupert, are determined to discover what the cunning Count is up to this time. Not that finding out would be much help… For how can they hope to foil the Count's plan to uncover the dagger's true potential, and awake Vlad Dracula himself…?

The Tall Tales of
Dracula's Daggers

The Return of the Count
(In which the Undead get out of bed…)

Gary Morecambe

SCHOLASTIC